WRITTEN BY KELLI ROBERTS
AND RICHARD BACULA

PUBLISHED BY WASTELAND.COM

# LETTING GO

ISBN-13: 978-1502310194
ISBN-10: 1502310198

# CONTENTS

# CHAPTER 1

When I was a little girl, my friend Marianna Gacy had a tarot card reader at her birthday party. The woman was dressed up like a gypsy fortune teller, wearing exotic colorful clothes, and both the woman and the cards stand out in my memory even today.

I was interested in fairy tales, in romance and true love, so I asked the woman about just that. I asked her about the boy that I'd marry, what he'd be like, when I'd meet him. I asked her little girl questions, and I got some surprising answers.

She laid the cards out in a strange pattern, then went through them one by one, explaining each card as she went through the progression.

I don't remember everything. I don't recall all the cards, or their positions, or all of the meanings, but I do know that some of the cards that came up were scary. There was one with a picture of the Devil, for instance. That one obviously wasn't good.

There was another card that depicted a tall tower being struck by lightning, a card that the tarot reader told me represented some kind of disaster, the kind of loss where you can't even repair the damage. You have to rebuild.

The good news was the final card, the card that showed my ultimate destiny. That card was a Prince, holding a stout wooden rod.

"The Prince of Wands," she told me. "A strong man, a man of discipline. Probably a school-mate, or a co-worker at a job you'll have. There may be some travel involved, you'll go places together. In order for the relationship to work out, you'll have to be brave, and you'll have to make sure that the two of you have clear communication between you."

That made me happy! I knew that I'd find my very own Prince Charming someday, and that we'd get to travel together, to have adventures.

I spent my teenage years dreaming about this man. Part of my mind kept trying to make different boys fit the reading. If a boy was into sports, I'd think that he was strong, well-disciplined, and I'd think, "Maybe this is him! Maybe it's time!"

Part of me always knew, though, that none of them were going to be my prince. They were just boys. I was looking for a man.

I didn't date much in high school. The fantasy of my prince was always better than the reality of drunken, groping high schoolers.

Part of the problem was that, starting when I was fifteen, I had to take a part-time job. Between that and school, I had little time for a social life.

My father died when I was still a baby. My mother did her best to raise me on her own, but money was tight, and we needed the extra income that I brought in.

I didn't have a bad life, but it wasn't exactly all that great either. Mother did the best she could but still it was a struggle and having three square meals a day was never guaranteed. So I kept working, year after year, through the rest of high school.

I never made it to college. My grades weren't quite good enough to get a scholarship, and the immediate need for enough money just to survive kept me working at dead-end job after dead-end job, until two years ago.

That was when I lucked out and landed a job as an assistant at a law firm. It wasn't entirely luck, though. What happened was that I ran into my old friend Marianna, and we caught up on each other's lives.

She had made it to college, and was studying law. She had an internship at the law firm Pendergast, Hartman, and Kent, one of those large firms that had been around for decades. They had offices all over the world, including one right here in Houston, and they were always looking for good people.

Marianna didn't have any pull, but she was friendly with some people who did, and she recommended me for an assistant position. I was nervous, but I apparently interviewed well because I got the job.

The Houston office where I worked specialized in high-stakes corporate litigation. That's where I first laid eyes on Jaxon Kent.

Every Friday, a large number of the workers would gather at the wine bar downstairs, on the first level of the enormous building where the PH&K offices were located. It served as a good way for people to get to know their co-workers better, as well as a chance for the lower tier employees to mingle with their bosses in a relatively low-pressure atmosphere. I say "relatively" because they were still your bosses, and even though most of them were laid back, it was always a good idea to watch how much you had to drink.

More than a few people put their jobs in jeopardy by getting a bit too tipsy at these Friday night get-togethers. There was one guy who crossed the line with his flirting, violating the anti-sexual harassment policy in a major way. There was another guy who puked on a partner's shoes. Then there was me, who after a few to many glasses of wine decided to take a chance on going after the man I'd been slowly become obsessed with over the last two years.

The first time that I saw Jaxon Kent was only a few months into my job. My immediate boss, Marcy Scarbaro, was a friendly woman who had been insisting since my first week that I join everybody for the Friday night get-togethers at the bar. It was one of those awkward situations where your boss wants to socialize with you, and between their personality and the fact that they're your boss, you eventually have to accept, even though you don't want to.

Marcy dragged me out to the bar, where I cautiously sipped my drink and tried to fade into the background while she told me stories about different court cases she'd been involved with. Suddenly, I found myself interrupting her, cutting her off mid-sentence to ask a question that seemed so important that it slipped out before I even had a chance to think about it.

"Who is that?" I nodded at the stunningly handsome man standing at the bar. The bar was full of men in expensive suits, but this one man stood out from the crowd as if there was a spotlight on him. I had never seen a man who looked that beautiful, that masculine.

By the time the question left my lips, I was already starting to turn a bit red, embarrassed that I'd interrupted my boss, and embarrassed that I'd shown such obvious interest in a man I'd never met.

Marcy blinked at the interruption, but as soon as she saw who I was looking at, she smiled. "*That* is Jaxon Kent."

"As in, 'Pendergast, Hartman, and Kent?'" I asked.

"No," Marcy laughed. "His great, great grandfather--or something like that--was a founding partner. Jaxon's just a senior associate. He'll probably make partner soon enough though."

My eyes widened a bit, even though they were already openly staring at the man.

"Is he…"

I wasn't sure how to ask the question. It seemed absurd, like asking if anybody owned the sunset.

"Is he taken?" Marcy was smirking at me.

"No, he's single. But believe me, you don't want to get involved there. He's got an endless string of girls already queued up, and… rumor has it, he's into some pretty strange stuff."

She leaned in close for that last part, dropping her voice to a whisper.

"Like what?" I was kind of intrigued, but from the way she said it I wasn't sure that I wanted to know.

"Bondage. Crazy stuff. Not for normal girls."

She seemed to realize that she was perhaps gossiping too much too soon. I hadn't been working for her that long, and she didn't really know me all that well.

"You didn't hear any of this from me."

She clammed up after that.

The little information that she had shared with me made me more wary of Jaxon, but it also made me slightly intrigued. What kind of bondage? What kind of crazy stuff?

As Marcy returned the conversation to more mundane matters, I kept stealing glances at Jaxon. I had images of lying on a bed, my hands tied together with that red necktie he was wearing, while he pushed up my skirt. I started to feel warm. I wondered if I was a "normal girl."

# CHAPTER 2

A couple months later, I actually got to meet Jaxon. Marcy introduced us. She did a lot of head-shaking about my continued interest in the man, but still took a great deal of pleasure in introducing us. She secretly mouthed the words "You owe me!" while I was shaking his hand.

His hand was distracting. He was being gentle with me, but his grip was firm. I could feel the strength in him, feel the sheer power of that hand, of those fingers. I stammered my name, even though Marcy had just said it. Jaxon smiled and said his own name back, as if Marcy hadn't already introduced us.

It was his smile, I think, that first got me. I'd seen him do it before, but only from a distance. Up close, it was amazing. His smile was so big, so genuine, and when he smiled you could see it in his eyes. It wasn't just a motion that his mouth was making, it was real emotion.

Or maybe it was his eyes. I'm a sucker for eyes. A good pair of eyes makes me go a bit weak in the knees, makes me go a bit dizzy, and Jaxon Kent had a great pair of eyes. Jaxon's eyes almost made me melt into a stupor. They were a certain shade of blue that the sky sometimes gets, a shade that made me think of flying kites as a child, or of that moment on an airplane trip where you look out the window, looking up instead of down, and you feel so completely immersed and free, so surrounded by that blueness that you feel like you're losing yourself, becoming part of the atmosphere, becoming a part of the planet. Or maybe I'm the only one who feels that way sometimes. I've never really discussed it with others.

Jaxon's hair was dark like the night. As I looked up at him, still shaking his hand, I wanted to touch his hair, run my fingers through it, muss up that perfectly groomed hair of his, not just for the tactile sensation but to see how he would react.

I realized that I'd been shaking his hand a beat or two too long. I blushed, and let go, stepping back almost with a stumble. I'd never had a man affect me that way before.

He must have seen it, must have noticed the kind of effect he was having on me. He probably got that kind of reaction a lot, looking the way he did, but he seemed to enjoy it. His smile grew slightly wider, almost becoming a laugh. It was as if we were sharing some kind of inside joke between us, one that I didn't really understand.

There was an easy confidence about him as if he was in his element, as if he owned the bar that we were standing in, as if he owned the world. When some man interrupted the moment by walking up and talking to him, Jaxon transitioned smoothly from his interaction with me to his new interaction. He gave me a slight nod of his head before turning away, as if to say, "Good. I've met you now, and it was nice. I will be seeing you again."

It was as if he was noting something special that he'd have time to get back to later. He was like a man who had opened a Christmas present, found the contents pleasing, but who had to turn his attention to the next gift. He would have time to get back to his new toy later, play with it at his leisure, because he knew that he owned it.

I had no idea who the man who interrupted us was, but I wanted to thank him for distracting Jaxon while I could slip away to the table I was sharing with Marcy and her friends. Part of me also wanted to kill him. I finally got to meet Jaxon Kent, to shake his hand, and this man ended that moment for me. It was both a pain and a relief to have Jaxon turn his attention away from me.

After that, I never missed a Friday night at the bar. I had just turned twenty-one, so I was new to drinking. I was enjoying the experience of getting to drink with my co-workers, and the regular socializing with them was growing on me, especially since I could hang out with friends like Marianna and Marcy. The main draw, though, was always the chance that I could see Jaxon again, the times where I'd get to talk to him, however briefly.

I knew that my interest in Jaxon was just a pointless obsession, that even if by some miracle he became interested in me, nothing could ever happen between us. He wasn't likely to risk status by dating a lowly assistant (no matter how well they treated us at the firm), and I wasn't willing to risk my job by trying to date a boss. I needed my job not just to try to pay my bills, not just to try to slowly claw my way out of credit card debt, but I was still sending money back to my mother on a regular basis, helping her out financially when I could. She needed me to have this job as well.

I couldn't help myself, though. When Jaxon and I ran into each other at the bar, when I got the chance to talk to him, to be around him, I flirted with him. I was hardly the only girl who did, and I was a lot classier about it than most. I kept the flirting light and friendly, the kind of flirting you do almost as a kind of politeness even when there's genuine interest.

He did the same with me, flirted back, to my amazement. He flirted with a lot of girls the same way, superficial and friendly, but sometimes with me I felt like he meant it, like he could actually be interested in me if things were a bit different. We developed a kind of friendly rapport between us over time, and I noticed that he spent more attention on me when we were at the bar than he spent on other girls. At least it seemed that way.

Early on, after I'd only met him the one time, they had a party to celebrate somebody's birthday. It was one of those little office parties, just cake and some soft drinks in the break room. I was still new and I didn't really know many people at work. I felt out of place, awkward, and I was still trying to keep a low profile. I didn't bother going to the break room for the party but instead tried to catch up on work at my desk.

I noticed somebody approaching, and I looked up. It was Jaxon, carrying two of those little plastic plates, each with a piece of birthday cake on them. He held one of them out to me.

"I saw you over here," he said, "and I thought I'd bring you a bit of cake. You don't have to be shy here, you know. We're all one big happy family."

He winked at me. I took the cake and blushed a little bit. Now I felt awkward for avoiding the party. He wandered off, picking at his cake with a plastic fork, but it felt so nice that he even noticed me. Most people wouldn't have. Most people didn't.

It was only later that I found out that he was the one they were having the party for. He took time out on his birthday to make me feel welcome, even though he barely knew me.

He wasn't kidding about the firm, either. They really did try to treat their employees like family. Before my job at Pendergast, Hartman, and Kent, I had a view of lawyers as having a kind of a high and mighty attitude. I pictured them as being arrogant, the kind of people who felt smugly superior to others, but it wasn't that way here. The firm tried to foster a true team spirit, to make everyone feel like they had an important role to play in winning each and every case.

Of course I didn't encounter Jaxon at work all that often. Our jobs didn't intersect or overlap regularly. There was this one time, though, when Marcy sent me to deliver some files to his office. The door wasn't entirely closed, so I didn't think to knock before I walked on in. I didn't expect him to be standing in front of his desk, bare-chested.

He'd obviously been changing shirts for some reason. There was a white shirt draped across his desk, and he was just leaning over to pick up a darker shirt from the chair next to him. He stopped. He looked up at me. He smiled that smile and walked over to take the files from me, as if his shirtlessness wasn't even an issue. That man seemed to feel completely at home, in control, no matter what the situation was.

I tried not to stare at the muscles doing interesting things under the skin of his forearms as he reached for the files. My limp fingers released the folder into his hands. I was feeling a bit flushed, and not just in my face.

"Thank you," he said. Then, after a moment, "Is there anything else?"

I realized that I was still just standing there, trying not to stare at his naked torso, at those lean, rock-hard muscles of his. I already knew that the man was well-built; I could tell it through his clothes, just by the way they hung on his body. Actually seeing him without a shirt, though, changed that knowledge from something hypothetical into something more concrete. It was like the difference between knowing that cars move fast and getting run over by one.

I couldn't look him in the eye, and I couldn't just stare at his chest, but I couldn't really look away either. I ended up just shaking my head and slowly backing out the door, feeling like an idiot. I considered that a victory. At least I'd resisted all of my urges to walk forward instead, to walk up to him and to touch him, to feel those firm muscles with my hands, to explore his body with my fingers, maybe with my lips.

Jaxon shut the door behind me, and I went back to my own workspace. I felt hot, almost feverish. I had this warm, liquid feeling down low, between my legs. I was wet. I didn't get much work done the rest of that day, and I didn't get much sleep that night. I'd never been so distracted by a man before, never felt so completely drawn to another person.

After that, my interest in him started to turn into a bit of an obsession.

# CHAPTER 3

I knew that getting romantically entangled with somebody from work would be a mistake, and I still wasn't willing to risk my job, not even after seeing so much more of what Jaxon had to offer. I needed my job, and I loved working there. My mom needed me to keep my job. I tried to ignore my own body but it wasn't easy. It kept trying to tell me that I needed Jaxon Kent more.

I kept things just as they always had been before. I stayed professional at the office, and I stayed flirty-but-friendly with Jaxon at the bar. I told myself that I was doing well, that I was keeping things normal, that my interest in Jaxon wasn't all that important. At the same time, I found myself trying to find out more about the man, to find out everything I could about him and his mysterious sex life.

As it turned out, nobody knew much more about his private life. Marcy couldn't tell me more than she'd said before, which was that he was into "strange stuff, stuff that a normal girl wouldn't have anything to do with." What exactly that "strange stuff" was, though, I couldn't find out.

Marianna had no problem helping me dig up information on him, and not just because she was my friend. I wasn't the only person in the office that was interested in Mr. Kent, and Marianna let me know that she'd had more than one or two fantasies about what he might do to her in the copy room, or on his desk.

She'd shared her thoughts about other men too, though, and she wasn't really graphic about it. I think she appreciated Jaxon's body, but I don't think that he was special to her in the same way he was to me.

When she mentioned his desk, I had a sudden flash of that day I walked in on him without his shirt. I had a brief vision of him telling me to pick something up off of his desk, and then when I was leaning over it, of him roughly forcing my chest down onto that desk with one hand while he put his other hand under my skirt. I imagined him pulling my panties off... no, of him just ripping them off of me, while I was helpless to resist. Then he'd lift up my skirt, and he'd...

"Getting warmer?" Marianna asked me.

I felt embarrassed for a second, before realizing that she had no way to know what I'd just been thinking. She was asking if my internet search was turning up anything about Jaxon's romantic history.

"Nope. I found a few pics of him with girls at different social events, but never the same girl, and none of them are actually mentioned as being his girlfriend or anything. All of them are lookers, though."

"Lookers?" Marianna smirked. "Or hookers? Maybe he only pays for it."

I had to laugh at that one. It was hard to imagine a man like Jaxon ever having to pay for sex, but then again if he was into some kind of strange kink, maybe he had to.

"Oh, shut up." I told her playfully.

The thought stuck with me, though.

Over time, that idea got more and more traction in my mind. Although Jaxon would flirt with girls from the office a bit, not to mention the female staff at the bar, we'd never seen him make an actual move on any of them. Marianna swore that she'd seen him leave the bar with girls before but couldn't remember who or when. I'd always left before Jaxon did, so I never had the chance to notice. I always called it a night pretty early, simply because I didn't want to end up drinking too much around my co-workers.

I started staying around later on Fridays, waiting later and later, until I was able to catch Jaxon leaving. He always seemed to leave alone. One time, on a whim, I followed him out, but he just got into big black car that pulled up and left.

I gave up after that, feeling a bit silly and childish. I didn't want to turn into a stalker, and it didn't look like I was going to find out anything interesting. So I pulled back a bit, stopped staying out so late in the vain hope that I'd unravel Jaxon's secrets.

Marianna had no such qualms. When we were children, she was the one who liked to pretend to be Nancy Drew or some kind of secret agent. She really liked that kind of thing, and I think she enjoyed the challenge that Jaxon presented.

Several months after I'd given up hope and tried to move on, Marianna told me that she'd been watching Jaxon as much as she could, and that she'd found something. I chastised her for not leaving the man alone, and for not telling me what she was doing. Then I all but begged her to fill me in on all the details.

There weren't many. Marianna had finally managed to catch Jaxon leaving the bar with a woman, and what she saw raised more questions than it answered.

Marianna had been coming out of the ladies' room when she noticed a tall leggy blonde strolling in through the doors of the bar. This woman didn't look familiar and she seemed a bit out of place in the bar, if only because she looked more like a model getting ready to walk the runway than a bar patron.

As Marianna walked toward her table, she noticed this woman approaching Jaxon at the bar. Marianna decided that this would be a good time to order a new drink. She happened to be standing at the bar, right behind Jaxon's back, when this woman greeted him.

The woman introduced herself as Stephanie Mayflower. Jaxon smiled, put his arm around the woman's waist, and they immediately left the bar together.

"That's weird!" I said. "What... was it like a blind date or something, where all he knew was her name?"

"Maybe," Marianna said. "Or an escort service."

I didn't like that idea, that Jaxon might be having sex with prostitutes. Part of me, though, found that idea more of a relief than the idea of a blind date. Really, I didn't like the thought of him having sex with anybody. Well, anybody but me. With prostitutes, though, at least there wasn't the issue of a permanent relationship. I wouldn't have to walk into his office on an errand some day and have him introduce me to his fiancée.

Marianna and I spent quite a bit of time speculating. But there just wasn't enough information to do anything with. That was until another piece of the puzzle fell into place.

This time I was the one who saw Jaxon with a woman. I had actually been talking with him at the bar just before she approached. It was the kind of idle chit-chat that we did from time to time, where I'd try my best to match his witty banter until I felt like my brain was going to melt out of my ear just from the sheer presence of the man. Then I'd excuse myself and return to my table.

It was difficult, because he had those eyes and when he talked to me, he'd look at me. When he looked at me, when I looked back at his eyes, I'd feel myself start to melt. He always looked at me as if he knew something I didn't, and I never knew whether it was something about me, about him, or both.

My conversation had hit that point where it was about to turn into stammering and blushing, and he seemed to get far too much delight when that sort of thing happened to me, so I wrapped up my end and turned around to go back to my table. That's when I almost ran into the pretty redhead who was walking up.

I had to stop short, right before our breasts would have collided and I'd have spilled my drink all over us both. We each apologized, and walked around each other. As I was walking away from the bar, cursing myself for nearly causing an embarrassing accident, I heard the woman say, "Mr. Kent? Hi, I'm Tiffany, Tiffany Mayflower."

By the time I got back to the table where Marianna was waiting, Jaxon and Ms. Tiffany Mayflower were walking out the door together.

"What the fuck?" Marianna let out a breath when I told her what I'd heard. "That's it. Those two girls aren't sisters. They can't be! It's got to be an escort service."

I didn't want to agree, but I couldn't see any other conclusion.

I tried to put Jaxon out of my mind after that, tried to tell myself that if he was the kind of man who would rather be with prostitutes than in a real relationship, I'd be better off putting my focus elsewhere.

When my mind would wander toward thinking of him during the day, I'd force myself to remember his little hobby in order to shock myself into snapping out of it. Instead, all too often I'd end up fantasizing about being one of the Mayflowers, one of the beautiful girls who had the freedom to walk right up to him, say their name, then spend the night with their naked body wrapped around him.

That's how messed up my mind was, how caught up in him I was. I found myself re-evaluating my priorities and morality. Prostitution was immoral, I knew that. But my mind was re-evaluating that standard.

My entire brain should have been telling me, "Prostitution is bad, Jaxon uses prostitutes, therefore Jaxon is bad news." Instead, some part of me started either thinking or feeling, "Jaxon uses prostitutes, Jaxon is perfect, therefore perhaps prostitution isn't all that bad."

In the end, I made peace with it. My thoughts and emotions found a kind of balance where I ended up not really thinking badly about Jaxon, or his hobby, but where it still changed my perspective of him enough for me to gain a little more emotional distance from him.

As time went by, I was able to reconcile that if he was into paying for sex, he wasn't right for me. We just wouldn't fit. I wasn't into that, and I didn't think that men would spend a lot of money just to sleep with me in any case.

My interest in Jaxon became less obsessive, and I was able to focus more on my work and other aspects of my life. It wasn't always easy. I tried dating a few guys that I'd met here or there, but the results were the same as in high school-- awkwardness, ineptness, and immaturity.

None of them seemed to be a real man--at least not in comparison to Jaxon. None of them had his level of confidence, or his ability to smoothly back up that confidence with action.

Still, over the next several months as Marianna and I watched the occasional new Mayflower first appear at the bar, then disappear with Jaxon, I managed to avoid being really jealous of them. Jaxon was a man who could afford expensive things, and that, I told myself, was all that they were: expensive things.

I fell into a kind of peace where I could be certain that even if Jaxon and I would never end up being a couple, at least he wasn't likely to end up dating anybody else either.

That peace fell apart on the day I discovered that the Mayflower women weren't actually prostitutes at all.

# CHAPTER 4

"**N**o," I told the receptionist in the polished marble lobby, "I don't have an appointment. Like I said, this is an emergency."

"I'm sorry, but Ms. Zanardi isn't seeing anybody without an appointment today. You'll have to come back tomorrow." The woman seemed apologetic but firm. She had her orders and was either determined to stick to them or incapable of finding a way around them.

I had started off quite polite, my usual somewhat shy and socially anxious self, but in my frustration I was becoming more firm, more hostile. It was weird, but this girl seemed to be responding better to that. Her words didn't change, but her attitude seemed to. Maybe it was her job. Maybe she was so used to being bossed around by others, that's what worked best with her.

I took a slow breath, trying to adjust my attitude. This woman apparently was used to being bossed around by powerful people, so being nice probably wasn't the right way to go. I had to be assertive, to be bossy. Well maybe not bossy, just confident. I found myself asking, "What would Jaxon do?"

"Ms. Scarbaro," I said, making sure not to refer to Marcy as my boss this time. I wanted to convey the impression that I had no boss, that nobody was in charge of me.

I had to make the conversation strictly about my authority over this receptionist, not about anybody else's authority over me. I looked her in the eye, trying to look at her the way that Jaxon did at people, as if I owned her.

I continued, "Ms. Marcy Scarbaro of Pendergast, Hartman, and Kent, sent me. This envelope has to be hand-delivered, by me, directly to Ms. Zanardi. Today. Right now."

It seemed to work. She looked a bit flustered, a bit worried. "But I don't see what--"

I cut her off. I had to push the offensive. I didn't like being this way, but I also kind of did like it. I generally prefer being more laid back, to let somebody else take the reins and responsibilities, but it was kind of nice being in charge for a change, seeing somebody else on the other end of the stick. I interrupted her mid-sentence, channeling my inner bitch in order to make the girl in front of me understand and submit.

"Well, you need to see. It's your job to see. You're the one who's in charge of making sure that the people who need to get in to see your superiors actually do get in, and to keep out the rest. If you can't see that I'm one of the people that you're supposed to let in, then you're not doing your job, Miss…"

I paused to read her name tag. It showed only her first name, but that was enough.

I suddenly realized where exactly I had seen this girl before, and what the context was. The words came out of me without really thinking about them, about what exactly they might mean, or that they might just make this encounter all the more awkward.

"Miss Tiffany Mayflower."

The girl's eyes went big, like really, really big. It was as if she were a mouse, and another mouse that she'd been sniffing noses with suddenly turned into a cat.

She didn't move, didn't speak, just looked at me helplessly. It's hard to stare directly into another person's eyes, to be that intimate with another person without flinching or blinking, but I managed to do it because that's what Jaxon would do. He wouldn't flinch and he wouldn't blink. He'd assume control whether it was in the courtroom, or in a fancy lobby, or…

"I'm sorry, Mistress." The girl's lovely green eyes dropped down, and her demeanor sort of collapsed. She was suddenly completely submissive in front of me, as if I hadn't just taken charge of the situation, but had taken complete ownership of her. My mind read that last part back. Mistress?

I didn't say anything further because she was using the phone, punching numbers into it without looking up at me. A weak inner part of me was scared, thinking, "She's going to call security!" I quashed that part, knowing that was not what she was doing. I just wasn't used to winning, that's all. Not this completely.

"This is Tiffany Majors," she said into the phone. "I have a priority engagement for Ms. Zanardi. Yes. Yes. This is that important. Okay."

She hung up the phone, then faced me without meeting my eyes. She almost flinched as she spoke. "I'm sorry. It'll be five minutes."

I probably should have quit while I was ahead. I probably should have given her a gruff nod, then retreated to one of the leather chairs over near the fake fireplace in the waiting area and looked at one of the magazines or books there. I couldn't help myself, though. I had to take advantage of this unique opportunity.

I gave her a brief glare, then softened a bit. The softening part was easy, because it was my more natural state. I was elated, but tried to sound barely satisfied. "I suppose that will do."

The girl gave me a brief, grateful glance, then turned her eyes down again.

"If I'm going to have to wait, though, I'll need you to keep me entertained with some light conversation." My mind was working frantically, trying to figure out how to keep up whatever bizarre bluff I'd managed to pull over the girl, while still getting the information that I wanted. "I believe you know Mr. Jaxon Kent? He works at the same office that I do."

Again, I was careful not to point out that Jaxon was my boss, that he was an attorney, while I was just an errand girl.

The girl seemed trapped, as if she thought the cat was going to let her escape, then she was suddenly skewered by a massive claw or fang. She didn't seem to know what to say, but she seemed to think that she had to say something. It was odd seeing somebody be this completely powerless in front of me. It was uncomfortable, but strangely… appealing.

"Yes." She said. Then she seemed to catch herself making some kind of mistake. She didn't seem to question how I knew that she knew him. Maybe she recognized me, or maybe she just assumed that I knew everything. "Yes, Mistress, I know Master Jaxon Kent."

Master, not mister. Just like I was suddenly Mistress. I was getting more questions than answers from her so far. I tried to figure out how to say this next part. "Can you… can you tell me exactly how you know him? How it works between the two of you?"

"I…" She became flustered, as if caught between two conflicting rules or directives. "I am not allowed to discuss my personal interactions with Master J."

"No, of course not." I prodded her more, as if I was being deliberately cruel. Everything I did had to seem deliberate. I'd rather this girl think that I was a complete bitch than to have her realize how completely in over my head I was. "But there are impersonal parts, parts that I'm allowed to know, parts that I probably already do know, but that I'd like to hear from you."

She seemed to consider this. She appeared to be wracked with anxiety, which made me feel sorry for her because I was normally the one who ended up feeling that way. At the same time, the power I had over her made me feel almost giddy. Was this what it was like for Jaxon, when he dealt with normal people? Or when he dealt with the Mayflower girls?

"Mistress Sophie lends me to him, you know. Sometimes when I've been bad, sometimes when I've been good, I meet him at the bar. I let him know who I am, tell him my slave name, then I'm his for the weekend."

I had no idea what to do with any of that. I had so many questions, but they all seemed too risky to say out loud, and I had no idea how to phrase them. I tried to smile enigmatically at her, then I nodded and went to the waiting area, carefully facing away from her so that she couldn't see my face turning red, and know how flustered and anxiety-ridden I was.

Very quickly, she announced that I could go up. She left out the "Mistress" this time, probably because she was speaking loud enough to be overheard if anybody was near. I got the envelope delivered to Ms. Zanardi, and Marcy was very pleased with me. She asked how I managed to get in there, because she knew that I'd have trouble without an appointment. I just told her that I have my ways.

It was good that Marcy was happy with me, because the rest of the day my work was off. I was sloppy, distracted. My brain was trying to absorb all the new information that it had, obsessing on different things that I'd been told.

The girl was "lent" to Jaxon, not "sold" or "rented." There was no mention of money, and from the girl's behavior I no longer thought that money was what any of this was about.

"Master J." Jaxon Kent was "Master J." The name sounded like a rap star, but not in this context. It was a secret name, like "Mayflower," only "Mayflower" was a slave name, and Jaxon was the opposite of that. He was apparently a Master.

The part that took up most of my mind, though, that even tugged at my heart, was the last part that Tiffany Mayflower said, that final phrase of our unusual conversation: "his for the weekend."

At first I couldn't wait to tell Marianna about everything. When I finally talked to her again, though, I found myself avoiding the subject. I hadn't exactly fallen down the proverbial rabbit hole, but I had at least stuck my head inside and I couldn't quite find the words to describe what I'd seen there, not to anybody who hadn't had a glimpse themselves.

Also, it felt like it would be a betrayal of Jaxon. I had found out enough secret information about him that this no longer felt like a game. It felt like an intrusion. What had started off as playful fantasy had turned into more of an invasion of his privacy.

It's one thing to know that a man is into something "dreadfully kinky," as Marcy had put it. It's another thing to know that he borrows slaves on a regular basis, to use for an entire weekend. I wondered if it happened every weekend.

I wondered how he used them. Surely it wasn't just to keep his apartment clean. I mean, he must have been having sex with them. That just seemed obvious. I wasn't sure how to react to that. Prostitution seemed somehow impersonal, like a business transaction. Slavery, though?

If it was real slavery, like illegal, non-consensual slavery, that was obviously wrong. This wasn't that kind of thing, though. Tiffany Mayflower didn't seem like she was an actual slave. She didn't seem like she'd been kidnapped or forced into anything.

Even at her most painfully, humiliatingly submissive moment during our interactions the other day, it seemed like part of her was almost enjoying it. As if she both hated and enjoyed being put into that kind of awkwardness. It reminded me of watching a child being tickled, where the child is obviously suffering and they want the person tickling them to stop, but they also wanted the torture to continue.

It reminded me of how I felt when I talked to Jaxon, when he'd look at me with those eyes, when he'd transfix me by casually staring into my soul.

Jaxon had slaves. Well, he borrowed them. Did he own any himself? If I was to break into his apartment, would I find a harem of beauties chained up there? I felt funny just thinking about it. I felt sick. I felt parts of me start to heat up. If I thought about it too long, some of those parts would start to moisten. Jaxon had sex slaves.

# CHAPTER 5

I tried to let it go. I tried to ignore it. I tried to think of other things. I tried to want other men. I tried to control myself.

I failed.

Part of the problem with being the only child of a single parent is that there's a lot of burden on your shoulders. As much as your mother might do to take care of you, you have to do a lot of taking care of yourself, and you have to do a lot of taking care of her whenever you are able to.

My life was always filled with things that I had to do, things that were required, and I always did them. I learned a great deal of discipline, of reigning in my own emotions in order to do whatever needed to be done. Mom needed my help with chores, so I did chores because they had to be done. Mom needed me to get a job, so I got a job because it didn't matter if I wanted to socialize with my friends--we needed to keep the power on.

At work, the business came first, and the customers came first, and my bosses came first. There was always something to do, something that had to be done, and I always did it because I had discipline.

Discipline is not the same, though, as self-control. Not exactly.

One of the problems I'd always had was in situations where nothing specifically *had* to be done, where I was left to my own devices, where I had to judge for myself when and where to stop myself. I'd grown so accustomed to people telling me what I had to do, to acting on whatever the biggest emergency was, that I was at my most dangerous in non-emergency situations, because that was when I didn't know how to behave. More than that, those were the times when I couldn't behave.

I could control myself for the benefit of other people, but I had trouble controlling myself for my own best interests. If my mom counted on me doing something, then I did it. If my boss or a friend counted on me to do something, then I did it. I didn't want to disappoint them, and I couldn't bear the thought of letting somebody else down.

But when it came to me? Somehow, that's where I lost it. When it was only my own interests at stake, that's when I seemed to either slack off or to go too far.

That's what eventually happened with Jaxon. I lost control and I went too far.

*

Roughly two years since I first got my job at PH&K, I made the mistake of drinking too much at the Friday night get-together. I'd seen other people make that mistake, and I'd always been careful not to do it myself. Then I somehow did it anyway.

I was trying out a new Riesling that evening, and I ended up tipsier than I meant to be. I wasn't really drunk, but I was pretty close. I wouldn't have been out of control, but when it came to Jaxon my control was already slipping.

I'd been successful at keeping any interactions between us more friendly-flirty than serious-flirty because I couldn't afford to lose this job. In my head, though, I had been losing myself for a while. I'd been fantasizing more and more about Jaxon.

I'd be talking to him about work, but I'd be thinking about what he'd look like naked. I'd be wondering what exactly he did with those slave girls he borrowed for weekends. I'd picture Tiffany Mayflower wearing a French maid costume, bent over Jaxon's knee so he could punish her for not cleaning the drapes. I'd picture him lying on a bed, shirtless, while I hand-fed him grapes. It was all silly stuff, but I couldn't get it out of my head, even when I was sober.

It got worse with proximity-- the closer I was to him, the more out of control my thoughts would get. I'd watch him speak, I'd find myself staring at those lips of his, and I'd want to just lean in and kiss him. I wanted to taste his mouth, feel his tongue. I wanted him, but I was powerless to get him. He had his Mayflower girls, and I couldn't compete with them.

I was coming out of the restroom that night, the last time I ever went to the Friday night get-together, the night my life changed forever. I was tipsy from the Riesling, and I wasn't even thinking about Jaxon. I was thinking about something that Marcy had said about wolves breeding with coyotes in the northeast. Wildlife was one of her passions, and I had come up with something interesting to say on the topic. It was clever and insightful, but the thought was knocked right out of me when I obliviously walked smack into a wall.

A lot of things happened at once. I bounced back off of the wall, rebounding like a half-hearted squash ball, and I suddenly understood that the Riesling had gotten to me more than I'd thought. I wasn't looking where I was going and I was off-balance, and now I was going to fall on my ass because I'd been careless with my drinking.

As I was bouncing backward, preparing myself to fall, I also noticed that the wall that I'd run into was somehow in the middle of the hallway instead of being on one of the sides, and that the wall was wearing Jaxon's finely-tailored business suit.

As the wall smoothly slid out an arm to catch me around the waist, I noticed what blue, beautiful eyes the wall had, and what a wide grin. It occurred to me that the wall hadn't felt quite like brick, that it felt more like meat, or like the kind of insanely firm muscles that were now supporting me as Jaxon Kent leaned forward slightly to pull me all the way back upright.

I had walked smack into Jaxon and had bounced off him like a June bug off a windowpane. He'd caught me, though, before I had bounced very far, and now I was in his arms. Well, in his arm. He really didn't seem to need the other one to support me.

He was looking at me with those eyes of his, gazing into me, and I gazed back. There was an odd beat where nothing else happened, where the rest of the world seemed to evaporate, and all that existed was our eyes.

Then we both grew conscious of the moment. I realized that Jaxon was breathing slightly heavily, even though catching me hadn't seemed to cause him any exertion. His arm was still around me even though I was now standing upright.

"Sorry about that." He was apologizing, even though I'd been the one who screwed up. "I should have been more careful, Ms. Munn."

I should have been thinking of my own apology. I should have been stammering out some confused, embarrassed admission that I was the one who was entirely at fault. Instead, I did something else, something that I didn't expect. It was the wine, it was his eyes, it was his arms around me. It was the moment. It was my weakness.

"Ms. Mayflower," I corrected him casually and politely, as if I wasn't giving it any thought. "Ms. Anastasia Mayflower."

Jaxon blinked with surprise, showing a motion and emotion that I hadn't been sure he was capable of. He let go of me. He stepped back. His eyes glanced around, perhaps to see if anybody was watching, perhaps to see if he could find any clues to what was happening.

"Mistress Sophie sent me." I found myself looking down, away from his eyes, the same way that Tiffany had done after I had called her by her slave name. I adopted the same kind of stance, the same kind of physical submissiveness, imitating the changes that I'd seen in her. It seemed like the thing to do.

Jaxon was quiet for a moment. I couldn't see him staring at me, but I could feel it. I could feel him judging me. My face started to turn red as my brain caught up to what the rest of me was doing, as the risk I was taking started to fully sink in.

I could lose my job. If he realized that I was bluffing, that I was trying to fake my way into his home and his heart, then he could have me fired. Somehow worse, he could laugh at me and walk away. On the other hand, if he didn't realize I was bluffing, what if he still laughed and walked away? The real Mayflowers could all be models. I wasn't ugly, but I didn't have any illusions that I could be a model. What if he fell for it but still turned me down?

We just stood there for another clenched fistful of excruciating moments. The silent anticipation was dreadful. I kept perfectly still, but my senses were on edge, sharpening, preparing themselves for whatever came next.

Then he spoke. He was calm and quiet, fully in control again. His voice sounded like it could have been discussing the weather, or the stock market. "I did not realize that you and I operated in the same circles."

It wasn't a question; it seemed like a challenge. In for a penny, in for a pound I supposed. "I'm new. I didn't know about you either, until tonight."

He seemed to consider that. He still seemed on guard, though, wary. "New? What's your threshold level? You couldn't be more than a two or a three. Sophie knows that I never bother with anything less than a four."

I bristled, although I had no idea what he was talking about. Whatever this rating system was, I disliked his assumption that I couldn't rate very highly. My mouth was still moving ahead of my brain, speaking out of indignation instead of intelligence. "I'm a seven."

"A seven?" My eyes were still low, but I swear I could hear his eyebrow arch as he spoke. His voice showed slight surprise, and something else. Could it be hunger?

"Seven." I almost whispered it, my voice growing weak, my heart beating rapidly. I wanted to undo it, to turn back time and make this never happen, just to reset things so that I was walking out of the restroom and managed to get back to the table without smacking into Jaxon. I couldn't change things now, though. I was helpless. It was all up to him now. I was at his mercy.

"She knows my rule about keeping my business life and my private life separate. She knows not to send anybody from the office to me."

I panicked a bit, but tried to quell it. Then I got distracted wondering about his phrasing. Were there other people at the office who were involved in this kind of thing? Who?

"I…" I couldn't think. There was too much happening too fast. "I'm a substitution. The girl she wanted to send couldn't make it. Mistress Sophie… well, she sent me in case you wanted to bend the rule a bit."

Another painful moment, as I simultaneously hoped that he'd send me away, and that he'd bend his rule. Then I felt his arm go back around my waist. His voice was low, thick with something that I hoped was hunger. "Well, let's go then."

We left. The big black car quickly pulled up out front, and we got into the back of it.

I never saw the inside of that wine bar again, nor the offices of PH&K. I didn't know it at the time, but this was the last moment of my former life.

There would be no going back.

# CHAPTER 6

The car sped along, moving deeper into the heart of Houston, past Interstate 610, into the area known as "The Loop."

"If Mistress Sophie sent you, then she has already instructed you on how to behave, but I'm going to go over it all again so there is absolutely no confusion."

I wasn't sure what to say, so I nodded. His eyes narrowed in annoyance.

"When you respond to me, you will address me as Master. The only words I expect to hear from you are yes Master or no Master, unless I instruct you to say something different."

"Yes, Master." I said. It seemed silly, but it was obvious that he expected me to do it. I didn't want to blow my cover now. Besides, my encounter with Tiffany Mayflower had pretty much prepped me for this sort of thing. I wondered if this was as far as it would go, if this would be like a normal date except he'd expect me to call him Master.

He nodded, satisfied with both my answer and my subservient demeanor.

"Because this is our first weekend together," he continued, "I am going to use this time to train you to my specific tastes. If you do not obey me you will be punished. If you do obey me, you will sometimes be punished anyway, for my pleasure."

I didn't like the sound of that. What kind of punishment did he have in mind?

As if reading my thoughts, he specified: "The punishments will take whatever form pleases me at the time. Typically you can expect to receive spankings, paddlings, and the other usual physical punishments, up to the type of thing that a Level Seven slave can endure."

A host of images suddenly flashed through my mind. I'd never been spanked before, even as a child. Paddlings? He couldn't really be serious, could he? If those were the start, what the hell was at the other end of the scale? I was starting to regret my bluster in declaring myself a Level Seven now that I was getting a better idea of what it entailed.

"My enthusiasm for humiliation isn't too high, so you shouldn't expect much in the way of abusive language, exposure to the general public, spitting, urination, or anything to do with feces. Don't expect it, and don't ask for it."

Don't ask for feces? No shit!

Jaxon's even mentioning that kind of stuff as being out of bounds was frightening because it was all so far beyond anything that I had expected. I wondered what other stuff would still be on the table. I wished I was home.

"There will be a safe word, of course. If at any time my attentions prove to be more than you can handle, then you can use this safe word to immediately end our weekend together. You will be returned to your home, or the location of your choice within reason, and our relationship will be terminated. You will never speak to anybody about the events of this weekend as per the non-disclosure agreement that you signed with Mistress Sophie, and you and I will never speak to each other again in any context."

Wait, what? If this weekend didn't work out, I could never speak to him again? Somehow, that hurt worse than the thought of losing my job, or even the thought of being humiliated by Jaxon's finding out that Mistress Sophie hadn't really sent me, that I was here on my own stupid initiative. My eyes must have gone wide at the thought of losing him even as a casual work friend.

I realized that he had kept talking while I was reacting to that last part, and that I missed hearing something important. I opened my mouth to speak, then remembered that I wasn't supposed to say anything other than "Yes, Master" or "No, Master" unless he instructed me to. Not knowing what else to do, I raised my hand.

He stifled a smirk. "You may speak, Slave."

"I'm sorry, Master." I might have forgotten to call him that, if he hadn't just called me his slave. "What was the safe word again?"

"Exodus," he said.

There was a beat of silence, and then he continued as if I hadn't interrupted.

"Do you understand these conditions?" He asked this firmly, looking me right in the eyes.

My brain pierced by his stare, I managed to stammer, "Yes, Master."

Something strange happened then. He was still staring into my eyes, and I managed to stare back, completely fascinated by him. His eyes were so blue, so deep. There were little flecks of color in them, different shades of blue within the blue. He had just the slightest tinge of brown in there, on the edge of his pupils.

Then I was staring into his eyes and I felt like I was sinking into the shiny blackness of them. More than that, I felt like he was sinking into me, like we were connecting somehow through our eyes, almost merging. I felt my mind shrinking. I felt like I was losing myself.

He was kissing me. His face had closed in on me while I was lost in his eyes. His lips were touching mine, parting them. His tongue was sliding inside my mouth as if he was tasting me, and I tasted him back.

I blinked, and our eye contact was broken. He blinked too, then broke off the kiss and pulled away from me.

"I'm…" There was something slightly soft about him then. He seemed almost confused. I had the feeling that he was about to apologize for kissing me, but then he remembered our situation. Then all of that disappeared and he became firm and formal again.

"I usually don't do that." It wasn't an apology, simply an observation. "I lost myself there for a moment."

It felt like one of us should say something, but neither of us did. Then the moment was interrupted as Jaxon's cell phone rang. When he answered it, I leaned back in my seat, ambivalent to be left with my own thoughts for company for a while. This was the first chance I had to think about what I was doing. I had managed to talk my way into Jaxon's car, and at this rate I'd soon be in his house, and then in his bed.

All it had taken was a spur-of-the-moment impulse to use the Mayflower name. I wasn't sure why I had said it. I mean, I had been lonely. I had been curious. I'd also been jealous, I think-- jealous of the

Mayflowers. I had wanted to have what they had. I wanted to be Jaxon's.

Was this what I really wanted, though? I'd had my fantasies about being with Jaxon, plenty of them, but those fantasies had involved nice dinners and fancy clothing. They had involved dancing and candlelight. None of those things seemed to be awaiting me if this evening continued, only… I didn't exactly know. Sex, obviously. Some kind of kinky sex involving bondage, something that regular girls didn't go for. That's not what I'd fantasized about.

I'd never really been all that keen on sex. I liked the idea of sex, but so far the reality had only let me down. I'd had a few encounters and they'd left me unsatisfied, feeling a bit cheap and used. The guys had enjoyed themselves and I enjoyed their pleasure, but I had never really been able to enjoy sex fully for myself. I had never even had an orgasm.

I had tried masturbating a number of times, when I could get the time alone in the small apartment that I'd shared with mom, and a few times since I'd moved out.

Somehow I just ended up sore and more frustrated than when I'd started. Like with the times I'd tried sex, the good feelings would start, the arousal would build up… then I'd just be left hanging there, unable to go any further. Eventually it would all fade and I'd give up. So I didn't think that kinky sex was what I was really looking for from Jaxon.

Which meant that I had to call this thing off, to shut it down. That's what I needed to do. It would be embarrassing to tell Jaxon the truth, that I had tricked him. It would be humiliating to let him know that I bluffed my way this far into his personal life, and that I didn't even really know why. I had to do it, though. The only alternative was unthinkable. I couldn't let my first date with Jaxon be a weekend as his sex slave. I just couldn't. I had to do something to stop this.

I sat silently in my seat for the rest of the trip, thinking about the kiss.

When the car finally came to a stop, it took me a moment to figure out why. We were there, at Jaxon's home. I knew that's where we were going. It's just that I'd expected Jaxon's place to be a big house in the suburbs, or maybe in a gated community. I hadn't expected Jaxon to live the penthouse of a refurbished warehouse.

I didn't even recognize it as a warehouse at first. The huge old building was one of those sprawling, oblong structures, like a giant rectangle, only I couldn't see all of it from where the car was. We were parked down near the south end of the building. At the time I couldn't see how long the building was, only how tall. It didn't look like a warehouse to me at all, not then. At the time, it looked like an enormous tower.

# CHAPTER 7

I'd often wondered about his home, what it would look like. I knew that he earned a lot of money as a senior associate and was rumored to have some family money, so it was a given that his place would be nice; what I wanted to know was how it was decorated. His office was always so tidy, so clean and well-organized. I suspected that his house would be the same.

As we'd approached the building, I had seen large bay doors around the side, but we ended up entering through a normal-sized door at the end of the building. It was one of those sturdy metal doors that looked like it was designed for security. Between that and the sturdy-looking brick walls, the place seemed like a fortress. I wondered what the crime rate was in this area. Was that the reason the place seemed like such a stronghold?

He pushed open the door and inside was a small, unused office area with an elegant antique elevator off to the side. The area was nice, well-kept and clean, but was rather sparse. It fit his personality perfectly.

He motioned for me to get in the elevator, then pushed the button for the top floor. When the doors of the elevator opened again I was completely taken aback. We were standing in a large foyer with ornate light fixtures and a beautiful cream carpet. In the middle of the room was a large marble statue.

It looked like Michelangelo's David. I knew it couldn't be, though. It had to be a replica. Still, it was a very, very good replica.

Jaxon was striding past the statue without a glance, headed toward two enormous green metal doors at the far end of the room. They looked old, like they were part of the original structure that never got updated, rather than a new paint job. Jaxon unlocked them and ushered me inside.

The entire top floor of the building was his, and it was nothing short of amazing. It had been converted into a luxurious penthouse suite that was a complete contrast to the building's plain exterior.

The ceilings had to be twenty feet high, and there were skylights everywhere. The floors looked like they were all hardwood, maybe oak, and there was a balcony on the far side of the enormous room we were standing in. I had assumed that his place would be expensive and stylish, but I never imagined that it would be so impressive. How much money did this man *have*?

Jaxon bolted the green doors shut behind us, and I began to get a bit nervous. What was I even doing here? What was he going to do to me?

Although I'd known Jaxon for years, this was the first time we were truly alone together. As soon as he locked the doors, he took off his jacket, hung it on the back of a chair, then turned to me with a serious expression.

"I'm glad that Mistress Sophie sent you to me. I've had my eye on you for a long time, Stasia." It wasn't the first time that Jaxon called me by that nickname. It wasn't the first time that I got goosebumps from it. It was just something that he had started calling me a while back. I'm not sure why. I liked it, though. It made me feel like I was special to him somehow.

There was a beat of silence. He was looking at me like I was supposed to say something. I remembered my role here, and I spoke. "Yes, Master."

Saying it made me feel like I was in an episode of *I Dream of Jeannie*, but Jaxon just nodded as if satisfied by my response. He was looking at me strangely, though. He led me to an overstuffed white sofa and motioned for me to sit down as he took the seat next to me.

"I'm sure Mistress Sophie has given you basic training, but I'm going to take this weekend to train you even more, to take you to new heights. I'll push the limits of your endurance, and bring you deep into a world of new experiences. Do you understand?"

Did I understand? No. No, I did not. What was he talking about? Formless images ran through my mind, tangled bodies of fog and flesh, wrapped in impossible positions, doing impossible things. I felt strange--scared, but also thrilled somehow.

Now was the time where I should say something. I should tell him that there's been a mistake, that I'd made a horrible mistake. The buzz of the alcohol had mostly faded in the course of the car ride, and a strange sobriety was setting in. The situation was so surreal, but reality had lost the pleasant fuzziness from the evening's earlier drinking, so the surreality seemed more menacing, more dangerous.

I formulated some sentences in my head. I put together strings of words that would help me break my inertia, to change the direction that this evening was taking me. I came up with a combination that I thought would work, and then I spoke.

The words that came out were not what I had planned.

"Yes, Jaxon. I understand."

Before I knew what was happening he was grabbing me, pulling me across his lap, holding me down. I struggled but he was just too strong.

He held my wrists with his left hand. He used his right hand to give me a sound swat on the bottom, making a loud SMACK sound as his bare hand connected with the thin layer of clothing that covered my body.

I ceased my futile struggling and let out a startled cry from the impact. A second later the pain kicked in, a sharp stinging pain in my buttocks.

He leaned over me and growled. "I told you to address me as 'Master.'"

I'd forgotten! This was what he'd meant by "punished." I opened my mouth to say something, to apologize, but I ended up just letting out another cry of shock and pain as his hand assaulted me once more, smacking me hard on my butt a second time, then a third.

He lifted up my dress, pulling it up to my waist, and suddenly my panties were the only thing between my flesh and the open air of the room. His hand started in on me again, smacking against my bottom again, and again. I let out more cries. I struggled.

I felt a bulge pressed up against my midsection. He was hard. He was enjoying this.

My attention was suddenly split, divided between the pain screaming through the lower part of my body and the sudden awareness of how close our bodies were. Even through the pain I was aware how good it felt to be held by him, to have my side resting against his flat stomach, to have my belly pressing down on the hard muscles of his thighs. It felt good to feel that other hardness there as well.

Adrenaline was rushing through my body from the pain. I found myself crying out with each slap, making a variety of sounds that I never knew I could make, trying to channel the pain that his hand was inflicting on me. I wanted this to stop.

I struggled. I kicked. I desperately moved my hips, trying to get away. It was all useless. He had me, and there was no escape or relief.

I could hear him letting out the occasional chuckle as I wriggled uselessly.

"Stop struggling," he told me. I complied, hoping desperately that if I obeyed him he'd stop hitting me, even though I knew in my heart that he wouldn't.

I felt his fingers slide under the fabric of my panties, felt him make a fist. He started to pull. I felt like a wishbone. My arms were being stretched out by his powerful left hand, and his even stronger right hand was pulling on my panties, making the fabric dig into my flesh. It was painful, but the mild pain was almost a relief compared to the spanking that he had been giving me.

I felt the muscles in his body straining underneath me, felt his stomach going even harder and flatter, felt his thighs tighten. He stretched the cloth to its limit, then relaxed slightly for a heartbeat, then yanked them up and to the side. The cloth dug deeper into my flesh, and then gave way, ripping into slackness as the gusset tore.

If I was a wishbone, then Jaxon got his wish.

I could feel the cool air on my body, on my most private parts. Then I felt his fingers. He gently stroked me there--down, then up. The tenderness was a strange contrast to the pain that he'd just been inflicting on me. His touch was electric. It was as if my body was more alive, more responsive than it had ever been. A startled gasp escaped from my lips.

Then the hand pulled away. There was the impact again as the spanking resumed. There were so many sensations: the smacking sound of his bare hand slapping my naked buttocks, the feel of his body underneath me, and pain like I'd never felt before.

As bad as the actual spanking was, the worst part was the time between each individual spank. My body was on full alert from the assault. It was ready for fight or flight, although it couldn't do either. My wriggling and squirming hadn't succeeded in avoiding any blows but my body was still trying to escape the pain, so it desperately wanted to brace for each impact.

My senses were straining for any signal of the next attack on my flesh, any sign that would let me know when to brace, but I couldn't see what he was doing, couldn't sense that awful hand arcing in at me until it was too late. He changed his pattern of strikes, came at me different ways, at different parts of my bottom, and I never knew quite when or how the next blow was coming. The anticipation, that was the most torturous part.

I endured this strange, violent mix of new sensations for what felt like a very, very long time. My flesh began to burn, feeling like I was on fire where he had been striking me. My emotions started to burn with a hate for this man. Why was he doing this to me?

Mostly, I was angry at myself. Why was I letting him do this?

I remembered that I could stop this at any time. I had a safe word. I could use it. That would mean blowing my cover. It would mean a lot of embarrassment, even humiliation, but it couldn't be worse than this, worse than him having me over his knee, spanking my bare ass like I was a naughty child.

I was torn, trying to decide which would be worse--letting this continue, or admitting my lies and ending it. The choice was taken from me before I could make it. Jaxon's hand once more stopped attacking me. His fingers once more found their way between my legs. Again, they gently stroked me there. This time, they also probed.

He had been taking more time between the strokes without me realizing it, giving my body more and more time to anticipate between blows. Not knowing when the final blow would come, my body was still on full alert from the spanking.

My nerve endings were all still straining for sensation, so when the sensations changed my heightened senses drank in the soft caress of his touch with an impossible thirst.

I moaned with inescapable pleasure as his fingertips brushed my intimate areas. I sighed as he slipped the tips of two fingers between my labia. I gasped in shock as they slid in smoothly, as I realized how wet I was down there.

"Yes." Jaxon said. He was pleased but unsurprised, satisfied as if at a job well-done. His fingertips slid back out, leaving my body hungry for more. They slid down and forward, finding my clitoris, spreading the wetness there. He slickly rubbed me there for a while. He pet my hair with his other hand. I felt myself squirming under his soft, skilled caresses.

I was confused. The spanking hadn't felt sexy. Well, the closeness was nice, being held against his body. Feeling him hard underneath me was sexy, too. But it was nowhere near sexy enough to outweigh all the pain he had inflicted on me. Nothing had ever hurt so much!

I let out another little gasp. I felt my hips moving, pressing against his fingers as they stroked me. Tears were leaking out of my eyes. But now that the spanking had stopped, and it was just soft touches, I had never felt so completely turned on.

It made me feel ashamed, like my body and my emotions were betraying me. I wasn't like this. I didn't get turned on by this kind of thing. I was a normal girl, not some kinky freak who liked being hurt. It was so completely confusing, so overwhelming, especially with my butt still burning with red pain, and my private parts singing with joy.

Jaxon stopped. He moved his hands away. "Okay. Stand up."

I did. Even that was a conflict of emotion. I wanted to slap him. I wanted to run. I wanted him to hold me. I was trembling. He was smiling.

"The first rule as my slave," he said, "is that clothing is a privilege, not a right. Not for you. Take off your dress."

I still wanted to slap him. I was hurt, angry. This was familiar, though. He wanted me naked. He wanted to have sex. I had done these things before, undressed for a man, had sex with him. Despite everything, I still desperately wanted to have sex with Jaxon, especially with my body so primed for him. The way I'd felt, squirming under his stroking, he could have taken me right there on the couch.

The worst is over, I thought. Now we get to the good part. This was horrible, but what happens next might make it all worthwhile. I started to remove my dress, then I remembered myself.

"Yes, Master." I no longer felt like I was in *I Dream of Jeannie*. Major Nelson would have never treated her that way! Although, come to think of it, sometimes <u>she</u> might have deserved it.

Soon my dress was on the floor at my feet. I removed my bra and dropped it as well. Then I removed my ruined panties, adding them to the heap. All I had left on were my high heels.

"You won't be needing these." He picked up the clothes from the floor and placed them in a neat pile on the sofa.

"Stand in front of me." He was looking at me now. I reluctantly obeyed. I was so completely naked. It made me aware of every one of my flaws. "Now, don't move."

I stood there, too scared to move a muscle. I never wanted to go through a spanking like that again. Jaxon exited through one of the doorways. I relaxed slightly. I got my trembling under control. I wondered what he was getting. A condom?

I thought about leaving. I thought about just grabbing my clothes, and running right out of there. I could find my own way home. I could find a new job. I could just run away.

Somehow, though, the need to see this through was stronger than the need to run. Whatever mix of my own emotions had spilled out, making me blurt out the word "Mayflower" to him back at the bar, whatever mix of desires for this man had made me increasingly obsessed with him over the years, needed to be fulfilled. Besides, I reminded myself, the worst is over now.

Jaxon returned with something in his hand. It was a thick leather collar, with small metal rings attached. He fastened it around my neck.

# CHAPTER 8

"That's better," Jaxon said. "Now you are beginning to look like a proper slave. We'll work on your behavior."

He attached a leash to the collar as if I was some sort of animal that he was going to take for a walk. "Get on the floor. Crawl on your hands and knees."

I hesitated. It seemed too demeaning for him to be serious. I wasn't an animal. That hesitation cost me. I felt his hand slap my tender bottom, hard. I jumped forward, then had to regain my balance because of the high heels. I got down on all fours.

What the hell was this about? I'd thought we were going to have sex now. He knew that I was ready. I knew that he was ready. Why this bizarre farce of having me crawl?

I again considered using the safe word. While I was mentally weighing my options, measuring my fears against my desires, I felt the collar yank on my neck. Jaxon had started walking and I'd missed it. The pressure was more on the sides of my neck than on my throat, but it had hurt a bit. Jaxon tugged on the leash impatiently.

I was angry with him, mad at him for doing all of this, for being so strange in his demands and in his lusts. Why couldn't he just treat me like a person? Why couldn't he want a normal girl? I dug into the carpet with my knees and my palms, refusing to go anywhere.

Jaxon frowned. "I see we are going to have to do this the hard way."

He walked back, smacked my butt again, harder this time. I yelped and moved sideways, defensively putting the side that he had smacked away from him.

He took two steps and smacked me on the other side. He sighed. "Turning the other cheek won't do you any good."

I spun around, still on all fours. I glared at him. He looked exasperated.

"What did I tell you about disobeying me?" He waited a while before I reluctantly answered.

"You said I would be punished." The words were soft, almost a murmur. He was going to spank me again, I realized. He'd warned me that he'd punish me if I disobeyed, and I did it anyway. I could have said the safe word, but instead I'd just been obstinate.

Another stinging slap hit my buttocks.

"What did you say?" he demanded.

Another slap landed before I realized my most recent mistake in a long night of mistakes.

"You said that I would be punished, Master." I said. The swats on my butt still hurt, but I think I was getting used to the pain. I still didn't like it, but it wasn't quite as sharp. Or perhaps I was just becoming accustomed to the piercing pain.

"That's better." He looked satisfied. "Don't make the same mistake again."

"No Master, I won't," I obediently replied. All I had to do was to play along with each request, to take this one step at a time. I could make it through this. I could. I just had to be careful, to anticipate what he wanted. I had to please him.

"You will have to be punished for your earlier refusal." He did not look disappointed at this. He looked almost eager.

Instead of tugging on the leash again, this time he just scooped me up in his arms. He was so strong. He lifted me effortlessly.

He carried me like a child into the next room, to a long, wooden table. It looked like an antique, but somehow it blended well with the modern furniture in the rest of his penthouse.

The table looked like it should be surrounded by knights or monks having some kind of medieval feast. It was empty, though. Oddly enough, there weren't even any chairs.

The only thing on the table were two objects in the center, on the side opposite from where we were standing. As we approached, I could see that they were some kind of leather cuffs. They appeared to be attached to the table with sturdy metal rings.

Jaxon set me down, then bent me over the table and slid my hands through the leather cuffs. He tightened some straps and I was stuck, held fast by the restraints. I instinctively tugged, trying to get free, but I was firmly trapped.

I was stretched across the table, my high-heeled feet still on the floor, my tender bottom completely exposed, helpless. The height of the table was such that I had to spread my legs slightly in order to keep my balance.

Jaxon ran his hand over my behind. I tried to turn around to see what he was doing, but the restraints wouldn't allow me that kind of motion. All I could do was to wait and see what he was going to do next.

That was when I became really scared. I had never been so helpless before, not even in Jaxon's iron grip on the couch. I had a flashback to any number of horror movies I had seen, and realized that I had never actually seen Jaxon with the same Mayflower girl twice.

They'd show up at the bar, they'd leave with him, and I'd never, ever see them again.

Well, no. I immediately realized that wasn't quite true. I did run into Tiffany again. That was what put me on the disastrous path that led me here. If Tiffany lived through her time with Jaxon, the man probably wasn't going to chop me up and put me in his freezer.

Come to think of it, Tiffany <u>had</u> lived through at least one weekend with Jaxon. She was younger than me, smaller than me, and she looked weaker than me. My pride kicked in. I had been intimidated by the beauty and sex appeal of the Mayflowers I'd seen, but I'd also felt a bit of scorn towards them. I'd felt like they might be prettier than I was, but that I was still better overall than they were.

This, I realized, was my chance to prove it. If I broke, if I used the safe word, not only would I have to face the humiliation of explaining to Jaxon how I ended up in his home tonight, but I'd also have to suffer the additional humiliation of knowing that I had broken in a situation where countless Mayflowers had endured.

I have many personal flaws. I have many virtues. I have some traits that seem to move from one category to the other, depending on circumstance. My stubbornness and my competitive nature are some of that other kind of trait. They'd helped get me into this fix, but they might just help get me out.

While I was mentally steeling myself for whatever was going to happen next, I heard several clues. I heard Jaxon's leather-soled shoes move across the room to the wall directly behind me. I heard a cabinet open. I heard Jaxon's shoes moving back across the room, moving around the table until he finally entered my view. He showed me what he had in his hands.

In one hand, he held some kind of paddle. I had never seen anything like it before. It was made of multiple layers of thick leather, like the kind they use for the soles of fancy shoes, stitched together with some kind of sturdy white thread.

In his other hand, he held a bamboo cane. The handle was wrapped in black leather, with thinner layers than the paddle, but it had the same white thread.

"Choose," he commanded me.

I shuddered. The Mayflower girls endured this? I remembered my mom telling me about a thing that happened back in the 1990s. An American teenager living in China had vandalized a bunch of cars. Like, really badly. He'd slashed tires, poured paint thinner on them, and he'd stolen a bunch of road signs as well. In China, they still cane people as punishment.

Caning breaks the skin. There is bleeding. I'd looked it up. As a girl, after mom had told me about it, I had become horribly fascinated with the subject.

There aren't geysers of blood, but it's not just a few drops either. The American government had pleaded on behalf of the kid, and the Chinese government reduced his sentence from six strikes of a cane down to only four strikes. The Chinese government felt like six strikes from a cane was sufficient punishment for somebody causing thousands of dollars' worth of damage. I wondered how many strikes Jaxon thought would be fit punishment for my refusal to crawl for him?

I didn't want to find out.

"The paddle." I said. Then I remembered myself and added, "Master."

Jaxon smiled as if I'd confirmed something that he'd already known. Then he looked at me, as if I was something of a puzzle.

"You have no idea," he told me. "How long I've wanted to have you at my table."

I was horrified. I was flattered. He'd fantasized about doing this to me? For how long? He'd taken notice of me, wanted me here, naked.

Jaxon left the cane on the table next to me where I could see it. He disappeared from view. I could hear his footsteps moving back around the table until they were behind me again.

My brain was screaming at me to quit this madness, to just stop. Just say the safe word before he could do any more harm to me. I gritted my teeth. Jaxon wanted me. I was going to prove to him that I could handle as much as the Mayflowers. I really hoped that they'd never chosen the cane.

I sensed movement. I heard a noise--the whoosh of the paddle moving through the air. I braced myself, but no impact came. I heard a second whoosh, then a third. What was he doing? Warming up? Or was he just trying to frighten me? If so, it was working.

As horrifying as the scene was for me, I tend to get bored easily. By the fifth whoosh, my mind had wandered back to the way that Jaxon's fingers felt on me, the way that they felt in me. I was still wet down there, I could tell. I still had tingling feelings where he had touched me.

What if he wasn't going to actually paddle me? What if he was just going to have sex with me, from behind, while I was helplessly stretched out like this? I remembered my workplace fantasies of Jaxon calling me into his office, of him bending me over the desk just like I was bent over this table and taking me from behind. Was my fantasy going to come true?

Even if he wasn't bluffing, even if he did use that leather paddle on me, surely he'd take advantage of the situation afterward. It occurred to me that other than that kiss in the car--that sweet, wonderful kiss--I hadn't really gotten anything from him. I mean, here I was completely naked in a well-lit room, on display for him. He could be looking right at my... at my private zone. My legs were still slightly apart, my hips tilted over the table, my ass raised up. I started to get embarrassed just thinking about what his view must be like. Yet he was still fully clothed.

He'd touched me, but I hadn't even touched him. I'd gotten a better look at him that day when he was shirtless in his office. My tingling increased just thinking about what he'd looked like that day. I became aware of my breasts lying flat against the ancient wood of the table. I imagined Jaxon's hands on them. I imagined him groping me as he entered me from behind.

That's when the first blow from the paddle landed.

I had thought that I knew what to expect. I had thought that this would be like the spanking, only worse. This wasn't just worse, though, it was also different. The spanking had all been done with a strong but light touch, Jaxon's hand stinging my skin. The leather paddle was thick and heavy. It didn't just smack my skin. It crashed into me hard, with almost a thud.

Where Jaxon's hand had stung my skin, making it hurt, making it burn, the paddle impacted deeper. I knew from the first strike that it was going to leave a bruise.

"Does that feel good?" Jaxon's voice was almost mocking.

I didn't respond. I didn't know what to say. I couldn't lie, couldn't just tell him that it felt good, even though that was what he seemed to want me to do.

He smacked me again with the paddle, on the other cheek this time. I winced, and my body bucked from the pain. I was going to have another bruise.

"I said, does that feel good?" He seemed almost angry.

"Yes, Master," I responded through gritted teeth. I could lie now, but I couldn't hold back the tears welling up in my eyes.

"When I ask you a question you will answer without hesitation or you will be punished." He was instructing me, like I was a disobedient grade-schooler.

"Yes, Master." I was getting good at saying that.

I could feel him run his hand over the still-burning flesh of my behind, then continue down my thigh. He wasn't exactly tender, but his touch was soft. He pushed my legs outwards, spreading them wider. If any parts of me had been concealed before, they weren't now.

"You do have a sweet little ass. You are going to make a great slave." He sounded pleased. It was both flattering and insulting, like I was some kind of prize animal that he'd just purchased, and he was inspecting the goods.

I reminded myself that he was doing what he was supposed to be doing. This was normal for him, his conduct was all perfectly appropriate. I was the interloper. I was the one who had snuck in uninvited. I was the one who had foolishly gotten in over my head, like a sheep in wolf's clothing during mating season.

"Jaxon." This was it. I'd had enough. I had to explain things to him, to make him understand. "Jaxon, listen to me.

"I didn't say you could speak." He was angry. I'd spoken out of turn. I'd called him by his name, not by his title. I started to cry.

"You will learn not to speak unless spoken to." He began spanking me with the paddle, and I lost the ability to speak. I lost all thoughts except for awareness of the sick, red pain that the paddle was inflicting on me. I full-out cried, tears streaming from my face. I prayed--and I hadn't prayed in years-- that my punishment would end.

Finally it did.

"Have you learned your lesson?" He asked the question simply, as if he had asked what time it was.

"Yes, Master," I murmured. Please, please, forgive me. Please stop. I tried to remember the safe word, but couldn't quite remember it. Something biblical. That was it: exodus. Departure. Escape. If I said it, I could leave. This would all be over.

Jaxon would never as much as speak to me again.

"I can't hear you," he said. The paddle smacked by bare flesh again.

"Yes, Master," I said. I managed to be louder this time.

"I don't want to hurt you, my sweet little slave. It's just the only way to ensure your obedience." He sounded almost kind. Almost. Why did I have to fall for this man?

I still couldn't bring myself to say the safe word. I still wanted to try to explain how much I was in over my head. I couldn't do either of those things, so I just responded with the only words that I knew he wanted to hear: "Yes, Master."

"That's a good girl!" He seemed genuinely pleased with me. He moved his hand over my buttocks, slowly, appraisingly. "Here is your reward."

He moved his hand lower and slipped a finger inside of me. I was still wet. The finger went in easily. A second finger joined it and they started probing, finding special spots within me that I hadn't even known about.

I was angry at him. I was furious at him for hurting me, for being the kind of man who would ever want to hurt a woman, but his fingers were quite skilled and my body was still on full alert, ripe and ready to assimilate any new sensations. I stifled a gasp as one of his fingertips pressed on a place deep inside of me, someplace that came to life with a glowing burst of pleasure.

Before the paddling, I would have eagerly welcomed him--any part of him--inside of me. Now my mind just wanted him to leave me alone, to go away and to let me cry. My body seemed to feel differently. My body didn't want him to stop. It wanted him to do more.

The fingers withdrew. Then one of the fingers entered me again. No, this was shorter. Thicker. Jaxon's thumb. His two fingers, still slick from being inside of me, found my clitoris. He squeezed and released, moving his hand back and forth. His thumb was sliding in and out of me, his fingers were slipping back and forth over my clit. This time I couldn't stifle the gasp.

He leaned over my body so that he could whisper in my ear. I could feel the heat from his body. He continued to move his hand, to tease me. No man had ever touched me that way before.

Jaxon knew the answer, he could feel the answer with his hands, he could hear the answer in that gasp that escaped through my lips, but he asked me anyway: "Do you like that?"

I knew the answer as well as he did: "Yes, Master."

"Do you want me to continue?"

"Yes, Master." I let out a soft moan and he began moving his hand faster. His thumb was pleasing and teasing at the same time. Its presence felt incredible, but it just wasn't quite enough to be fully satisfying. The sweet, slippery friction as his fingers glided over my clit was just amazing. I felt pleasure building up inside of me, sweet erotic sensations that felt like they were getting ready to explode. I felt like I was getting close to something, like that pleasure was turning into a pressure that was about to release.

The pain was still there. My buttocks still burned and stung. My arms ached from being locked in this position. The pain was fading into the background, though, as Jaxon's fingers worked their magic.

"You are a naughty girl, aren't you?" He sounded like he was smiling.

My hips were moving now, as best as they could. My body was meeting that thrusting thumb of his. I was grinding myself on his fingers. I couldn't deny his accusation.

"Yes, Master, oh God, yes." It was getting hard to talk, hard to think. My nipples were hard, rubbing against the table. I felt a loosening, an uncoiling somewhere below my navel and between my hips. I realized what that building pressure was. For the very first time in my life I was going to have an orgasm. I couldn't believe it.

"Are you going to come, you naughty girl?"

"Yes! Yes, Master!" My breathing was ragged. I was right on the edge.

He pulled his hand away from me entirely, and I was left hanging on that edge that I so desperately wanted to plunge off of. I let out a wordless cry of frustration.

"The thing is," he said. "I didn't say that you could come. You are my slave and you will come only when given permission to do so."

I couldn't believe it. I couldn't believe that he could bring me so close, so screamingly close, then just leave me hanging like that. He really was a sadist.

"Would you like to come, my slave?"

"Yes, Master." Yes, yes, oh, God, YES! Yes, I really, desperately wanted to come. I needed to come. I felt like if I didn't have an orgasm soon, my body would simply implode.

"In that case…" He trailed off, and his fingers returned to their previous position.

I groaned as his thumb slid back into my welcoming body. I could feel every millimeter of it. My body was so sensitive at that point, I swear, I could almost read his thumbprint.

The fingers found me, rubbed my little hood, rubbed the tiny bud beneath it, and I was immersed back into a world of satisfying, slick sensation. He tortured me a bit more. I could tell that whenever I got close, he'd slow down, or change up.

Minutes went by, minutes of the most erotic pleasure that I had ever known. I wanted it to never end. I wanted it to finish; I wanted that orgasmic bliss that I had been denied my entire life, that explosion of pleasure that was dancing teasingly around the edges of all my senses.

Then, finally, it happened. Jaxon could sense it. He kindly gave me permission right before it happened.

He said the words, "You may come now, slave," then an arc of pleasure shot from my clit to those special spots that he was touching inside of me, and that arc formed a lightning bolt of overwhelming bliss that shot up my spine and exploded in my brain.

The sheer power of it was too much to contain, and I had to scream the pleasure out of me while my body thrashed in my restraints. Every muscle twitched and danced, and every fiber of my body cried out in the physical joy of orgasm.

I kept crying out, and my brain started to melt down. Random thoughts, memories, and ideas blinked in and out of my head as my neurons kept exploding within me, like a series of tiny mushroom clouds. I forgot to breathe, then I remembered again, and I took in a deep gasp of air.

My mind slowly returned to me. I could think again.

That was it. That was an orgasm. That was what I had been missing out on for my entire life. I was too ecstatic to feel cheated by those lost years of pleasures never had, and the tears streaming from my face were tears of unbridled happiness. They were tears of completion.

"Oh, my slave." Jaxon's voice was filled with faux pity that almost masked his own happiness, and what sounded like significant pride. "Did I say that you could stop coming?"

His hand kept moving. His fingers and thumb kept rubbing and probing. I felt a kiss on my lower back, then a nip of Jaxon's teeth on one of my bruised buttocks. Then I exploded all over again, and again, as Jaxon forced more and more pleasure into me, until finally I couldn't take any more, and reality itself became a seemingly endless series of waves, of eternally cresting and falling pleasure.

At some point I must have passed out. I must have actually passed out from it all, because I only have vague memories of Jaxon carrying me down a hall, through a doorway, and setting me on a bed.

# CHAPTER 9

I don't know how long I was out, but when I woke up I was confused. I didn't know where I was. I didn't know what had happened. My body hurt all over, but especially my buttocks. I felt like I had run a marathon, then lost a brutal fight.

Bit by bit it all came back to me, what had happened the night before. How I'd had too much to drink. How I'd bluffed my way into Jaxon's life, and into his house. How I'd been stripped, collared, cuffed to a table, and beaten. I remembered how I had been at the mercy of a man who I thought I knew and trusted, but he turned out to be a violent monster.

True, I was somewhat to blame, but I was only to blame for getting into this mess, for falling prey to his desires. He was to blame for having them. He was the one who wasn't normal.

I also remembered the pleasure. I broke into a grin, but immediately stopped. My face hurt. Had he hit me in the face? No, I remembered. I had smacked myself on the table during one of the orgasms. Oh, my God. I remembered the pleasure.

I had been about to crack. I had been about to give up on my crush, my obsession with Jaxon, my job, my interest in men entirely. I had been about to use the safe word and just give up on it all… then Jaxon had given me my "reward," the carrot to go with the proverbial stick, and what a sweet carrot it was.

But oh, how brutal that stick was. I had some serious thinking to do.

I realized that I was hearing footsteps approach from the hallway. That must have been what woke me. The footsteps were getting louder. Not knowing what else to do or what to say when I saw Jaxon, I lay my head down, closed my eyes, and feigned sleep.

The door opened. The footsteps stopped but I felt movement in the air. The floor must be carpeted. I felt the coolness of a wet cloth on my forehead. It startled me into opening my eyes, blowing my plan of pretending to sleep until he went away again.

He was looking down at me with those beautiful blue eyes of his, eyes that seemed so innocent. He had a look of tender concern on his face, which I found difficult to understand considering the thrashing he had given me. How could he be such an odd mix of wonder and horror? How could he beat me, then bring me to screaming orgasm, then tend to my wounds the next day as if I'd merely suffered some kind of accident?

"In time you'll learn, my sweet," he said, his voice gentle and caring. "Once a punishment has been administered, you're absolved of your misbehavior and it won't be mentioned again. I forgive you for all your misbehaving."

I cringed. He didn't know all of my misbehaving. He didn't know that I had lied my way into his home. I suddenly realized that if he ever found out he'd probably consider that a much bigger transgression than simply forgetting to call him "Master" or speaking out of turn. I remembered that bamboo cane, and I shuddered.

Jaxon didn't seem to notice. He was busy undoing the handcuffs that had joined my wrists behind the wrought-iron bars of the headboard. I'd been handcuffed? I hadn't even woken up enough to notice. Why had he handcuffed me?

As soon as the cuffs were off, he joined me on the bed, scooping me up in his arms and holding me tightly. It was like afterglow had come for him the next day, and now he wanted to cuddle.

I became more aware of my surroundings as we lay there together. I noticed how soft the sheets were and how fluffy the pillows were. My bruised body appreciated the soft comfort. It was nice, lying there together, in spite of my soreness and pain.

He leaned in and kissed me. It was tender, sweet, and passionate like in the car last night. His tongue tasted of coffee and milk, and I realized that I was hungry. His mouth also tasted like him, and I enjoyed the flavor.

I couldn't fully enjoy the kiss, though, because I was still physically and emotionally sore from the beating he gave me the night before. Also, I was still very much attracted to him, but now I was also afraid of him.

I wanted to kiss him, but I was also afraid that if I didn't kiss him I'd receive another punishment. I mean, I could always use the safe word, always exodus my way out of his life entirely, but I still didn't want to have to do that. So that fear tainted the kiss.

We kissed for a while, and I managed to lose myself in kissing him. His tongue was skilled, and his lips were soft and strong. I still felt exhausted, and I let myself drift away and just focus on the kissing. It had been a long time fantasy, after all, kissing Jaxon, lying in bed with him. If I could have just skipped the horrible parts of last night, it would have been just like I always imagined. But I didn't skip those parts, so it wasn't.

"I'm so glad that Mistress Sophie sent you." He was practically beaming. "I've wanted you for so long, wanted to teach you so many things. You're going to find the balance between pleasure and pain."

I did not want to find out more about the balance between pleasure and pain. I just wanted to go home. I just wanted to retreat, to have time by myself to sort through all the overwhelming things that had happened to me last night. I had already learned enough about the balance between pleasure and pain. I preferred the pleasure.

Jaxon slid his hand underneath the soft sheet, cupping my naked breast. That's when I remembered that I had no clothes on. I had been naked in Jaxon's bed (well, a guest bed in his house), kissing him. Part of me rejoiced at getting to live out this long-time fantasy, but like the kiss, it was tainted.

If only we could have ended up here differently. If only I hadn't had that perverse impulse at the bar, hadn't told him that I was a Mayflower.

His hand on my breast felt good. His touch was strong and sure, just like he was. He kissed me some more, his fingers playing with my nipple until it had been teased achingly erect, then he lowered his head, placed several soft kisses on my breast, and then took my nipple into his mouth.

He sucked on it, caressed it with his tongue. I closed my eyes, sweet pleasure welling up in my breast until a thin strand of it moved down, connecting my nipple to my lower anatomy.

After a time, he moved his head to my other nipple. I wondered if we were going to have sex, and if we were, if it would be tainted too. In the meantime, I enjoyed the sensations that Jaxon was giving me.

We didn't have sex. Instead exhaustion overtook me and I fell asleep in his arms. I don't have any idea how long he lay there holding me, but I remember the feel of his body. He was solid, strong, and warm. I had never enjoyed sleeping with a man before, not really. I always ended up feeling smothered, claustrophobic. Perversely, I just felt safe in Jaxon's arms.

# CHAPTER 10

When I opened my eyes, sunlight was pouring in through a window. Jaxon was gone. I was alone in the big bed, and I struggled to sit up. I missed Jaxon's presence. I also kind of hated him. I was torn between conflicting emotions.

My body ached all over, but especially my buttocks. I slowly took stock of all the pains in my body, making a visual inspection as best as I could. Yes, I had bruises. I couldn't see all of them, but the ones that I had seemed to be doozies. They were kind of black in the center, with yellow on the outside, and purple somewhere in-between that was hard to pinpoint.

As I performed my self-examination, I could hear Jaxon singing in another room. It was some song that I didn't recognize. Sounded like something operatic. I caught just a snatch, but I didn't understand the words:

> "*L'amour est un oiseau rebelle*
>
> *Que nul ne peut apprivoiser,*
>
> *Et c'est bien en vain qu'on l'appelle...*"

He actually had a lovely voice, though I think he was singing in a lower register than it was written for. There was a lot that was lovely about him, although I'd seen the ugly side too. I had no idea how this weekend was going to end.

Actually, I had a lot of ideas, too many. Very few scenarios had any kind of happy ending. Even in the best of them, it was going to be weird seeing him at the office after all the things that he did to me last night.

I considered the possibility that I'd have to get another job. I'd hate to leave Pendergast, Hartman, and Kent, but I started to think that it was just going to be too strange to see Jaxon Kent day in and day out after all of this.

The smell of fresh coffee brewing in the other room brought me back to reality. I wanted a cup, but was afraid to call out to him and ask. Before long, I heard his footsteps coming towards the bedroom and soon he appeared at the door, carrying a large tray. He balanced the tray on the bed and smiled down at me.

"Good morning, my sweet little slave."

He was beaming, as if we'd shared a night of passion and tender moments. Well, actually, we'd had both of those things, but he was acting as if that had been all that we'd shared.

"Good morning, Master."

I remembered to call him that. It was starting to be second nature to me. I didn't think that was a good sign. Shouldn't a healthy relationship be between equals?

"I thought you might like some breakfast." He beamed at me, then kissed me on the forehead. Whatever else I was feeling, I liked the feel of his lips on my skin.

He sat on the bed. I started to reach for the tray, but he swatted my hand away from it.

"Don't make me cuff you again. You'd look too pretty, all stretched out and helpless like that, and who knows what would happen."

He smiled as he said it, as if he were casually flirting at the bar. I didn't want to be cuffed again.

He poured two cups of coffee and asked me if I took cream and sugar.

"Cream but not sugar, Master."

He added the cream, stirred the coffee and held the cup up to my mouth so I could drink. I did so, gratefully. It was weird that he didn't want me to use my own hands for this, but I was thirsty and I needed the caffeine.

There was a plate of croissants on the tray. He picked one up, tore a piece off and spread it with butter and jam, then fed it to me. Piece by piece he fed me the croissant, stopping only to wipe my mouth with a napkin.

It started to make a kind of sense. He wanted me helpless, completely dependent on him. It was weird, but it kind of started to make me feel special, pampered. It simultaneously felt like he was a slave feeding me grapes or whatever, and that I was some kind of creature that was incapable of feeding myself, like a baby bird.

The food was good and my empty stomach was grateful but it still felt strange. While we ate, he also handed me a small container with some pills. I recognized one as my birth control, but I wasn't sure what the others were. I looked at them closely, fearing what they could be. He must have noticed my suspicion.

"That's just a multi-vitamin. The larger clear one is fish oil. It's to enhance your immune system and help reduce inflammation."

It was strange to think that my torturer was concerned with my health and well-being, but I swallowed the pills and thanked him nonetheless. I didn't like that he must have gone through my purse to get my birth control pill, although it did at least mean that birth control was a priority for him. Some guys I'd met didn't think about it at all, just leaving it to the woman to protect herself.

"Do you need to go to the restroom?" He seemed genuinely concerned.

"Yes please, Master, I do." As soon as he asked, I realized that my bladder was quite full. I'd had a bit to drink last night, with no bathroom breaks.

"You may take your time in there. Have a shower, wash your hair, and so forth." He spoke like a gracious host, permitting a guest a rare luxury. "However, there is no lock on the door. As my slave, you have no right to privacy. I can and will come in as I please."

"Yes, Master," I replied, mostly concerned with emptying my bladder.

"The bathroom is through that door over there." He motioned to a door on the other side of the room. I wasn't happy about the lack of privacy, but there wasn't much that I could do about it. All I could do is pray he wouldn't come in while I was on the toilet, although I had no idea why he would even want to.

When I had finished using the potty, I stood up and looked around the bathroom. There were large full-length mirrors hanging on the walls, giving me a view of my bruised and beaten body from all angles. It wasn't pretty.

My buttocks were now colored with a dark rainbow of hues, from an ugly yellow to brown, with a bit of purple in between. That paddle had left its mark. I was still glad that he hadn't used the cane.

My muscles were sore, too. I'd been stretched, bent, cuffed, and otherwise used in ways that my body simply wasn't used to. I felt like I'd been through a wringer. I decided to take him up on that offer of using the shower.

The shower was amazing. It was essentially a large tiled alcove the size of a walk-in closet. It was separated from the rest of the bathroom with a wall made of glass bricks. Standing in the shower area, it was a pretty roomy area, and it seemed even more spacious from all the light coming through the glass wall.

I was used to a dingy tub and shower that darkened a bit as soon as I pulled the curtain shut, but this? This was amazing. It felt like I was at a spa.

I got the shower running good and hot, and I stepped in. The water stung and burned, but at the same time it felt very, very nice. My body relaxed, and the rushing water slowly cleared my head, soothed my aching muscles.

I stepped out of the spray after a while, grabbed a bottle of expensive-looking shampoo, and sudsed up my hair. Some kind of pleasant, unidentifiable scent drifted down at me from the shampoo, and it felt nice on my scalp. I stepped back into the spray and rinsed, watching the suds flow down my naked body, washing away into the drain.

There's something cleansing about showering, not just for the body, but for the soul. I felt as if my worries and concerns were flowing down the drain along with the shampoo bubbles and the water.

There was a bar of fancy soap as well. I picked it up and stepped out of the spray in order to lather up. That's when I saw Jaxon standing in the entrance to the shower area. He was completely naked.

It had been so long since I'd seen him with his shirt off that I'd actually forgotten how good he looked. I'd replayed that day over and over again in my fantasies, but at some point along the way I think I'd started to assume that my memory of his body was more fantasy than fact, that he'd become larger than life in my head, more beautiful in my mind than he was in the flesh.

Looking at the man standing naked in front of me, I realized that my memories and fantasies hadn't done him justice. His eyes, his grin, his shoulders and pecs, his lickable little nipples, his washboard abs... By the time my eyes had gotten to his waistline, to that sharp V of muscle that pointed down from his navel to his groin, I was absent-mindedly stepping forward, my hand outstretched toward him as if to touch him, to grab him. It wasn't a conscious thing--it was pure instinct.

He just looked at me, as if wondering what I was going to do next. I have to admit that I was curious about that myself. I didn't have time to decide, so I let my body and my instinct make the decisions for me. I let my attention be directed downward, right where that V of muscle was pointing, to the thatch of dark pubic hair, to that part of Jaxon that I'd so longed to see. The man was beautiful everywhere.

My hand kept reaching out, following my gaze, and the next thing I knew, my fingers were curling around his hardening member, lovingly caressing his length. I was finally touching him.

My emotions churned about wildly, and I realized that this moment was why I was here. This was why I'd told him that I was a Mayflower. This was why I'd never said the safe word. I wanted him. I wanted to be naked with him, and I wanted it so badly that I was apparently willing to do anything just to have him.

All the pain that he inflicted on me melted away like so many suds down a shower drain, and the memory of all the joys that he'd given me flooded into my mind, washing out all other thoughts. The slice of his birthday cake. The jokes, flirtations, and easy companionship at the bar. The kiss in the car. The unbearable pleasure he'd given me with his hands last night. I had an overwhelming urge to give him pleasure in return.

I sank to my knees in front of him and looked up at him towering over me. He had a mild smile on his face. I wanted to change it to a grin, or to a moan. As my knees touched the tiles, I had this odd feeling of rightness, like this was where I belonged.

I just looked at him for a moment, just drank in the sight of those secret places that I'd longed to explore. I felt his weight in my hand, felt the softness of the thin layer of skin that covered that delicious hardness. My other hand reached out, reached under, and gently caressed that pouch of tender flesh that held his testicles. His skin reacted to my touch, tightening, drawing in closer to his body.

With hardly a conscious decision on my part, my head moved forward, and my lips parted. My tongue probed out, licking the small slit at the end of his shaft. There was already a slight presence of slippery fluid there, something almost completely tasteless, but compelling. I wanted more of it, wanted to taste it in my mouth.

I flicked my tongue out to taste and caress the underside of his crown. My mouth opened a bit wider, and I took the tip of him between my lips, savoring the feel of his flesh.

I sucked on him, gently at first, then a bit harder. I moved my head slightly, forward and back, my taste buds rubbing sweetly along the underside of his crown. I did this for a little while, just took my time and enjoyed the feel of him, enjoyed the way that broad arrowhead of flesh felt against my tongue, the inside of my cheeks, and against the roof of my mouth. Then I wanted more of him.

The muscles in my jaw stretched wide to take him in, and I could feel the end of his shaft moving deeper into my mouth until it hit the entrance to my throat. I gagged slightly and slid back a bit until things were more comfortable. Then I focused on licking, on sucking, and on moving my head slowly back and forth.

I had my hand still on his shaft, and I made a fist around the base of his erection, gripping him tightly. I moved my hand along with my head, using my fist as a kind of stop, so that I couldn't take enough of him inside of me to make me gag again.

I ran my other hand up his leg, feeling the power in his lean muscles. I caressed my way up to his inner thighs, then used my fingers to tease and explore the pouch of soft, wrinkly flesh at the base of his shaft. I realized that he was shaved there, and that the rest of his pubic hair was neatly trimmed.

Then his hand was touching the back of my head, his fingers tangled in my hair, securing his grip on me. Physically, it was nice, but I was nervous about what he might do next. I was afraid that he'd push my head forward, forcing more of him into my mouth than I could handle. I'd had guys try to do that before. I didn't like it.

He just held me, though. His grip was firm, commanding, but he was still letting me move the way that I wanted to. It made me feel secure somehow.

Encouraged, I took a bit more of him into my mouth and was rewarded with an increase in his breathing. Over time, as my mouth sucked and slid over as much of his length as I could handle, those sexy little noises he was making turned into soft moans, then into groans.

I was doing this for him because I wanted to please him, but I was starting to get turned on myself. The feel of him, and the taste of him, and the sounds that he was making... it was all too much. I could feel myself getting wet, and not from the spray of the shower.

There was a point where I could feel him growing larger in my mouth. His hips were moving, thrusting forward in time with the movements of my head. The noises he was making were getting louder and louder.

I knew that he had to be close to coming. I was excited. I had never made a man come this way, just using my mouth. I eagerly pushed on in spite of the aching muscles in my jaw.

The grip on my hair tightened, and his groans turned into ragged gasps and a wordless shout of exultation. He came.

My mouth was filled with thick fluid as he came, and it startled me. I had known what was coming, so to speak, but I'd never actually experienced it before. It was sudden and strange. The taste wasn't unpleasant, but the slippery, sticky texture of it was a new experience, and my body didn't quite know how to handle it. I gagged, coughed, and pulled my head off of him. His hand released me.

I turned my head, spitting out the fluid that was threatening to choke me, and after some more coughing, I calmed down.

"Are you okay?" Jaxon asked me. There was concern in his voice, but also something else.

"Yeah." I said, then remembered myself. "I mean, yes, Master."

"Good," he said. Then I felt myself being pulled roughly to my feet. I looked at him in surprise, then felt myself being pushed against the wall, my breasts up against the cold tile.

His hand slapped one of my buttocks hard, then the other one. There was a series of quick, angry slaps that made my flesh first sting, then burn.

"You must never reject my seed." His voice was stern. "When I come in your mouth, you must swallow, or I will punish you."

Seed? Seriously? I suppressed a giggle, managing to look serious as I told him, "Yes, Master. I'm sorry, Master."

I was sorry, too. Not enormously sorry or anything, but I pictured how I would feel if a guy had gone down on me, then gagged and nearly vomited. It wouldn't feel very nice. I'd try to be better prepared the next time.

It occurred to me that this man had just hit me multiple times, and only a second or two later I had to fight off a giggle. I knew that he could have spanked me much, much harder than he had. It had stung, but it hadn't been too bad. It was a token punishment.

Also, it told me that I was adjusting. I was getting more used to him punishing me. That thought seemed strange and alien in my head.

As my mind worked on adjusting to this new information, to the idea that I was acclimatizing to this kind of bizarre, kinky discipline, Jaxon stepped forward and hugged me briefly. Then he stepped back again and pulled me into the hot stream of the shower.

We stood there, and Jaxon ran his hands over me, caressing my body. I was already aroused from seeing him, from having him in my mouth. My mind was replaying the sensations of him coming in my mouth, and my brain was rejoicing that I had given Jaxon Kent such a powerful orgasm.

I felt myself grinning, and I felt almost like purring as Jaxon ran his hands over me and through my wet hair. He nuzzled softly at my neck. He was acting surprisingly sweet and gentle.

He guided me back out of the water, then grabbed a bar of soap. He worked the soap in his hands until he got a good amount of suds going, then he proceeded to lather up my entire body with that exotic-smelling soap. It was nice. He was pampering me.

He cleaned me thoroughly, every part of me.

It was strange, tickly, to have him run his soap-covered hands down my backside, between my cheeks, rubbing soap over my anal entrance. I'd never had a man touch me there. It seemed dirty and embarrassing, but I let him do it.

If he wanted to wash me there, I wouldn't stop him. I didn't want to get punished again. Also, a part of me secretly enjoyed it. Although not as much as when he washed my breasts, and my private area.

By the time Jaxon had me entirely clean, my senses were tingling. I was ready for more. I was ready for sex. My body was aching for him.

I was ready to return the favor, to soap him up and get him clean. I was looking forward to running my lathered hands over all his muscles, over all of his body. Instead, though, he sent me away so that he could wash himself.

"Go back to the bed and lie down. Wait for me there."

I complied.

On the way out, I caught my reflection in the full-length mirror on the door. Specifically, I caught a glimpse of my backside. I was surprised to see that my buttocks were a deep pink, almost red. It was from the spanking, I realized.

I ran my finger over the reddened area. It was sore and sensitive. My flesh there still burned, and my nerves were still somewhat on alert from Jaxon's assault on me, in spite of the calming shower. While there was some tenderness, the sensitivity felt nice as well. It was as if for the first time ever, my body was coming to life.

I thought about how that had happened the night before, too, how after he spanked me my body was on full alert, and how this had heightened the pleasure Jaxon had given me with his fingers.

"Red alert." I murmured to myself. Then I turned and walked out the door.

# CHAPTER 11

I went back to the bed and collapsed face-down on top of the sheets. My mind worked to understand all that had been going on in the past twenty-four hours, what I'd gotten myself into. I kept having little flashbacks of the pain that Jaxon had given me, then I'd have flashbacks of all the pleasure that he'd given me as well. Then I think I slept.

I woke up to a sensation of pleasant warmth. I felt hands on me, smoothly gliding over my body with a sensual slipperiness. I realized that Jaxon was there, sitting on the bed next to me. He was rubbing some kind of oil onto my skin.

Whatever it was smelled nice, and it felt even nicer. Pretty soon he had my back, shoulders, and arms pleasantly oiled and massaged, and he started working on my tender hindquarters. The oil mixed with the burning sensation there, dulling and soothing it.

"That's nice," I said without thinking. I was still in a daze from my brief nap.

I was rewarded with a sound slap to the region that he'd been touching so nicely a moment before.

"Don't tense up, it will only make it hurt more. You need to learn to relax and accept your punishment."

His voice was low and soothing, as if he had never hurt me, as if he could never hurt me. How could he be so gentle and sweet one moment and so brutal the next?

"Yes, Master." I wished that I could talk to him, just talk to him like he was a regular person.

He returned to the task of massaging my body, working the oil into my buttocks, then into the crevice between them. His oiled fingertip lingered at the entrance to my anus, and I was afraid that he might decide to explore, to slide it on in. He didn't, though, and I felt a mixture of relief and disappointment.

His hand moved down, between my spread legs, massaging the flesh around my sex. He worked his finger up and down the length of my wet folds for a bit, eventually spreading my lips, then gently rubbing my clitoris. I couldn't help it--I moaned and pushed against him, wanting more. He pulled his hand out and spanked me.

"You are a greedy little thing, aren't you? You need to learn to appreciate what I give you." His voice was stern again, but lighter than before. It was as if he was playing some kind of game.

He spanked me again, harder than he had in the shower, and I knew by now my behind had to be several shades of red. It stung. It hurt. I could feel the heat emanating from my skin. My senses tingled. I was on red alert.

"Yes, Master." Somehow, the spanking only made my arousal stronger.

I felt his erection pushing up against my thigh, and I realized that he was still naked from the shower, just as I was. I had been without clothing so long now that it was becoming second nature.

As much as his hand was hurting me, my body still wanted him inside of me. I instinctively arched my back. His hand swatted me again, this time slapping against my sex.

"You are such a dirty little slut." His words were chastising, but his tone was one of admiration. "Look at you, begging me to fuck you."

I didn't respond. What could I say? He was being crude, but he was right. I wanted him to have sex with me. I wanted him to fuck me.

He spanked my ass again.

"Say it," Jaxon commanded. "Tell me what you want me to do to you."

I let out a yelp when his hand came down on my bare flesh again.

"Say it!" He was smiling sadistically. He knew what I wanted, but he insisted that I say it aloud, that I admit it to him, to myself, to the world.

I wanted the spanking to stop. I wanted him inside of me. The cheeks on my face started to blush as red as the cheeks that he was spanking. I managed a soft murmur: "I want you to... have sex with me, Master."

He spanked me again. "Say you want me to *fuck* you. Say it like you mean it."

This time I spoke much louder. I could follow orders. "I... I want you to fuck me, Master."

"What makes you think that you're worthy of it?" He spoke the words, and I suddenly realized that it was a secret fear. As much as I wanted him, I didn't feel like I deserved him.

"Please, Master. I promise I'll be good." I wasn't used to using profanity when talking about sex. I wasn't used to things being dirty. I wasn't used to begging. I said it all anyway, because it was all true. "I want you to... fuck me. Please, fuck me!"

The spanking stopped. His hands parted my butt-cheeks, then I felt the sensation of his fingertip on my anal entrance, probing. It was strange, tickly. It was intrusive. His fingertip started pressing into me, just a little, like a cat in a doorway that can't decide whether it wants to go in or out. Wait, not a fingertip. It was his thumb.

It was arousing, I had to admit. It was maddening. Part of me just wanted him to slide that thumb into me, to get it over with. The other part wanted him to move his hands away entirely.

My mind was quickly spinning out of control. The feeling of his large cock pushing against my leg, his thumb gently probing my asshole, it was all just so exquisite.

He kept his thumb there, teasing me, and he moved his fingers down to explore my sex. He teased my other entrance with his fingertips, then moved his slick fingers down to my clitoris. He trapped my clit between two of his fingers and started moving his hand in slow circles, my tender bud trapped in a wonderful friction.

I gasped.

He pulled those fingers off of my clit. He moved them up slightly, slid them between my inner labia. He slid them inside of me. I felt my body clench around the intruders, but I was so turned on that there really was very little resistance.

He moved his fingers in, and out. He found those special places inside of me that he was so, so good at finding. When he slid his fingers in, his thumb would start to pull away from the entrance to my ass. When he slid his fingers out, that thumb would start pushing forward again, threatening to truly enter me instead of just lurking in the threshold.

It was such a mix of sensations. My buttocks were still smoldering, the oil dampening down the earlier burning sensation. My body was enticed and repulsed by what his thumb was doing. His fingers were teasing, playing, stroking me into a slow frenzy.

It all drove me wild. I could barely stand it. This man was amazing--scary, but amazing. I never knew quite what he was going to do to me next.

As his fingers worked their magic inside of me, that thumb started probing deeper. Each time his fingers withdrew, that thumb grew a little bolder, until I could feel my body relaxing, opening up. My body was inviting it inside. With excruciating slowness, the thumb eventually accepted that invitation.

Once his thumb was inside of me, his rhythm changed a bit. Now, instead of the thrusts of his thumb and fingers alternating, they joined into one motion. His fingers slid into my vagina at the same time that his thumb slid into my ass. I was being penetrated twice with each thrust of his hand.

His other hand smacked me on each of my butt-cheeks, just soft slaps that barely stung. They were more of a shock than a sting. The shock made things more intense, but not really more painful.

Then he slid his other hand, the hand that had just spanked me, underneath my body, snaking its way past my belly, until his fingers found my clitoris. Now I was being penetrated in two places, and my little bud was being exquisitely teased.

I lost myself to the slowly building pleasure. My thoughts started to slow, and my body felt like it was on fire. My nipples rubbed against those soft sheets as I writhed under Jaxon's hands. I could feel my nipples harden, the fire spreading through my breasts. I began letting out soft gasps, a pressure valve for all the steamy sensations that were building up inside of me.

I was going to come. It was something of a shock, because in all my life it had only happened once before. Granted, that was last night, with Jaxon doing the kind of thing to me that he was doing now, but it was still a new and unusual experience for me.

Then I remembered Jaxon instructing me not to come without his permission. I remembered the punishment. I felt anxious, almost panicky.

"Master," I managed to gasp. It was difficult to form words. My body didn't want to talk, it just wanted to come, it wanted to explode in the kind of pleasure that Jaxon had given it last night. "Master, I'm going to come. May I come?"

"You'd better not," he warned me. "I forbid it."

That did it. For some perverse reason, having the pleasure *forbidden* pushed me right over the edge. My body clenched on his fingers, and on his thumb. My hips ground down on his other hand, rubbing my clitoris against him. The fires in my breasts and my loins all merged, exploded, and I was suddenly twisting my body in ecstasy, my gasps turning into shrieks and moans.

With each shockwave of bliss, my body would twitch and twist, but I was pinned in two places by Jaxon's hands, by his fingers and his thumb inside of me. The more I moved, the more sensation there was, the more I was aware of him inside of me.

The thumb was particularly present in my awareness. It felt huge. Its presence somehow augmented the sensations that his fingers were causing, making everything more intense.

I couldn't take it. I screamed, clawed at the bed, tried to get away. Jaxon leaned on me with his shoulder, holding me down while his hands forced more and more pleasure on me. I couldn't stop coming, and I couldn't escape.

He kept his fingers on my clitoris, but he pulled his fingers out of me eventually. He used his free hand to spank me, over and over again. It hurt, but I was still so aroused that it was a different kind of feeling. The pain mixed in with my continuing orgasm, blending into some new third sensation that was a mix of both.

With his fingers no longer inside of me, with the spanking, I slowly wound down, came back to reality. His fingers still played with my clit, but I stopped coming and was able to lie still except for the occasional aftershock that made my body jerk or twitch.

The spanking stopped. His fingers stopped. He pulled away. I just lay there, trying to breathe, trying to think. I could feel Jaxon looking down at me.

After a while, he sat up. "You came without permission again."

"Ayuugh," I said. I couldn't quite talk yet. I couldn't even remember what I had just tried to say, but I remembered what I hadn't said. I focused, then said it as clearly as I could. "Master."

I felt completely limp, drained, and satisfied. I was tired, sore, and happy. I could feel Jaxon turning me over, and I couldn't even really help him or fight him. I was too limp.

Jaxon used the handcuffs to secure my hands. I was lying on my back, naked, my legs slightly spread. My arms were stretched out over my head, shackled to the ornate headboard.

"What did I tell you about coming without permission?" Jaxon asked me.

"You…" I focused. "You said that I would be punished, Master."

"Yes," he said. "And you will be. This infraction will go into your punishment book. I will take note of each time you disobey me, and at the end of the day you will be punished for each and every transgression. There will be no exceptions, and there will be no excuses. Every time you disobey, every time you hesitate to obey a command, and every time you talk out of turn, it will go into the book for a future punishment. Do you understand?"

It didn't really seem fair, but I was too satisfied to complain. Besides, complaining would probably be considered "talking out of turn."

"Yes Master," I said.

My good mood was starting to dampen. Why did he have to be like that? Why did he have to want to punish me for being a person instead of a toy? I felt insulted that as much as he seemed to appreciate my body, he didn't seem to be interested in my mind. I should be able to talk to him.

Jaxon seemed satisfied with my answer. He stood up, nodded, and he left the room. I lay there silently, trying to be mad at Jaxon, but mostly just enjoying the afterglow.

I heard him moving around in another room for a while. Eventually, he reappeared. He was freshly shaven, dressed in a nice suit.

"I have to go out for a while," he said.

"Yes, Master."

I was confused. He was going somewhere without me? Surely he wasn't just going to leave me here, cuffed to the bed, while he went out to do God only knows what.

He reached into his pocket, and for a moment I expected him to pull out a key to the handcuffs. Instead, he pulled out a pair of wooden clothespins. I had no idea what to make of that, but I couldn't ask him. I remained silent, waiting to see what he was going to do next.

He grinned at me, a devious sadistic grin. He leaned over and put his mouth on my right breast. I closed my eyes and let out a contented sigh. He sucked at my nipple, teasing it with his tongue until it was erect.

A sweet ache blossomed in my breast, and little sparks of pleasure started shooting outward, some of them finding their way to my groin. Just as I started to get really turned on, though, Jaxon pulled his head away from my breast entirely.

I opened my eyes. Jaxon was just staring at me, looking at my breast admiringly. I looked down to see what he saw. My nipple was fully erect, large and red. It ached for more of his attention. He leaned over to my other breast, took my other nipple in his mouth, repeating the process. By the time he was done, both my nipples were like diamonds on my chest, hard, shiny, and beautiful.

Then he reached out and clamped one of the clothespins on each of my nipples, grinning all the while. It hurt, a lot. At first it was just a pinch, then it was a sharper pain, almost needle-like. I took a sharp breath, trying to shake off the pain, but the pain didn't shake. It just stayed with me.

I had been so focused on the pain that Jaxon's voice startled me: "What you need to understand is that you are mine now. Your body is mine, all of it, to do with as I please. Your mouth is mine. Your sweet little tits are mine. Your tight little pussy is mine. Your ass is mine. I'm going to take you when I want, where I want, and how I want. I'm going to do whatever I want with you, because for this entire weekend, you belong to me."

He gave this some time to sink in. I tried to assimilate what he was saying, but the pain was distracting. Also, I couldn't wrap my mind around belonging to another person on that level. I couldn't understand my body not being just my own.

He continued. "You are my slave. You are my property. These clothespins are there to remind you of that fact while I'm away."

He paused again. He reached down, grabbed me firmly by the chin, and he made me look directly into his eyes. A shiver ran down my neck.

"Of course," he said, "you are free to leave at any time, even while I am gone. You can still say the safe word, and you can remove those clothespins, and you can walk out of my door, if that's what you truly want to do. Just remember that if you break, if you leave, you can never come back, and I can never speak to you again."

At the time, that was starting to sound like a pretty good deal. The pain in my nipples was turning into a burning sensation, although a great deal of sharpness still remained. I kept hoping that my body would adjust, but the clothespins just kept hurting me.

"I will know if you cheat." He stated that as if it was a simple fact, a certainty. "If you take off the cuffs and you remove those clothespins from your pretty little nipples, I'll know about it. If you do that, and you're still here when I return, I'll punish you for it."

I tried moving my breasts, tried adjusting my body to a better position, but no matter how I adjusted, the clothespins had my nipples trapped in their wooden jaws.

He reached up toward my hands, flicking some tabs on the cuffs that I hadn't noticed before. "These tabs will let you out of the cuffs. Notice that you can reach them with your thumbs if you try. Of course, since you're a level seven, I expect that this won't tax your limits very much."

He leaned down and kissed me on the forehead. "I won't be gone too long, my slave. Try to be a good girl in my absence. I have big plans for us."

Jaxon walked out the door, shutting it behind him, leaving me alone with my pain.

# CHAPTER 12

Once I heard the front door shut, I couldn't hold it back any longer. I cried. Tears started leaking out of my eyes, then they started streaming, and then I was sobbing. This was all just so fucked up!

I was naked, handcuffed to a bed, with clothespins painfully clamped on my nipples. I couldn't believe this was happening, not to me. I'd never imagined that I could be involved in something like this. I wasn't into this kind of kink. I wasn't into pain.

Yet here I was, and I was here somewhat voluntarily. I had trapped myself in a no-win situation where my only choices were to keep letting the man that I had a crush on torture me, or to lose him forever, with the added bonus of humiliating myself by explaining that I'd been so pathetically attracted to him that I'd conned myself into his bed by pretending to be something that I wasn't. This wasn't me. I was a normal girl, not a slave.

I cried for a while, but it was futile. It didn't make me feel any better. It didn't make the pain in my nipples any less.

That was the thing about the clamps--they didn't change. They just hurt, and they kept hurting.

When I was spanked, the initial blow hurt a lot, but the pain almost immediately receded into a sting and a burn, and it faded over time. Most pain was that way--it hurt a lot at first, but then it went away. This wasn't going away. The clamps were still there.

I swore out loud from the pain. What kind of asshole was Jaxon anyway? Why would he do this to another person? Sure, I'd told him that I was a 'level seven,' whatever exactly that meant, but why would he want to do this to somebody even if they could handle it? Even if they could enjoy it?

Why the hell couldn't Jaxon just be normal, like I was? Why did he have to be such a sadistic freak? I swore again. It still didn't help.

Time passed. I couldn't tell how much time, because I couldn't see a clock, I wasn't wearing a watch, and God only knew where my cell phone was. Jaxon had gone through my purse, apparently, because he'd gotten me my birth control pills, but I had no idea where my purse actually was.

I could look for it. That idea occurred to me, and it had a strong appeal. I could undo the cuffs and look for my purse. Jaxon said that he'd know, but could he really know?

I looked around the room for a hidden camera or something. I made a game of it. My nipples were still in pain. The game didn't help. I had to make a decision.

Was Jaxon really worth all of this suffering? Hell, no! Nobody was. I needed to get out of here. I needed to swallow my pride and just leave. He'd eventually find out that I'd lied to him in any case. I was going through all this torture just to delay the inevitable. Except if he found out while I was still here, while I was still his 'slave,' then he'd want to punish me.

I didn't want to find out what his punishment for lying was. I remembered the way the cane looked, lying on the table in front of me, while Jaxon paddled me. I shuddered. The clothespins moved, causing a slight spike of pain.

I moved my right thumb, using it to find that little tab that would release my wrist from the handcuffs. The cuffs were padded, but it was still slightly painful twisting my hand around to the right position.

My thumb touched the tab. I remembered Jaxon saying that if I left, I could never come back. I remembered how Jaxon had looked in the shower, how he had felt in my mouth. I remembered how he had rubbed me down with that scented oil that still clung to my naked skin. My thumb left the tab.

The clamps still hurt, but I'd made it this long. I could make it a bit longer while I thought this out. I didn't want to do something irrevocable. I didn't want to make any more mistakes.

I tried to think, but the pain made it difficult. It was still so omnipresent. No matter what I did, or what I thought, the pain was still there.

More minutes passed. I hadn't managed to come to any conclusions, or to even really think about things on any productive level. I kind of just gave up and laid there in the pain, hoping that things would get better, but feeling like this would just go on forever.

Eventually, I committed to the fact that I wasn't going to let myself out of those cuffs. I wasn't going to walk out the door to freedom. I didn't want freedom, not if it meant losing Jaxon. Even though I would probably lose him anyway, I managed to admit to myself that I wasn't going to give up on the insane course that I was on. I was going to see this through until the end.

Once I made that decision, I tried to make the best of things. I tried to enjoy the pain. People did enjoy this, apparently. I tried to make the sharp sensations into something pleasant, into a kind of pleasure.

It was still just pain.

More time passed. It was unimaginable, but somehow I was enduring it. I couldn't escape the pain, but I wouldn't let myself leave this situation. I couldn't embrace the pain either--it just hurt too much.

Eventually, my mind devolved into a kind of primal, whimpering self that was ready to grovel at the feat of… of whatever. Of Jaxon, if he ever came back. Of somebody else, if they showed up.

Of the pain itself, I think. It was like some ancient, primeval part of my reptile brain was taking over, like some superstitious, cowering part of me was assuming control. Like I was being controlled by some remnant of ages and evolutions ago, when kneeling and submission was a potent part of human survival.

After what seemed like an eternity, I heard the front door open. After what seemed like another eternity, Jaxon finally walked into the room. I was ecstatic to see him, like a dog whose owner finally returned from a long, long journey.

His face lit up for just a second when he saw me. Well, part of a second. It was like a tiny bit of emotion slipped past his careful guard, as if he was pleasantly surprised that I was still there.

"Please, Master!" I nodded my head at my tortured breasts.

"What?"

He was teasing me. That sadistic grin was back in place. He knew full well what anguish I was in.

"You want me to remove the clothespins?"

"Yes, Master, please."

"I suppose I can do that. If you have learned your lesson."

"I've learned my lesson, Master." I spoke through gritted teeth. I had almost adjusted to the pain, but now that the possibility of release had arisen, the pain seemed more unbearable than ever before. "Please."

Jaxon grabbed each of the clothespins, releasing them from my nipples. I let out a cry of pain as the circulation returned. It almost hurt more having them removed than it did putting them on.

My nipples hardened as blood flow returned, changing them from a pinched, bloodless white to a deep, rosy hue. In spite of the pain, I was struck by how pretty the change was.

Jaxon was staring, admiring my nipples with a hungry gaze. He leaned forward, gently kissing first one rosy little jewel, then the other. His mouth was soft, warm, and delicate, but the contact still hurt a bit.

He pulled his head away, admired my breasts again, then reached out with each hand and pinched both of my nipples. There was a lot of pain, but there was also something else, a kind of... not pleasure, really, but a sensation of erotic intensity.

I gasped.

I didn't like the pain, but that other part? Yes, please! It had sent a jolt down my torso, to my lower regions. My body reacted: loosening, dampening, readying itself.

I realized that I wanted Jaxon, really wanted him, right then and there. I was handcuffed, though, so there was nothing I could really do about it. I just had to lay there helplessly as Jaxon teased my breasts, alternating his fingers and his mouth.

Soon I was squirming on the bed, this blend of intense sensations making me writhe and moan. The pleasure grew in spite of the pain, or perhaps because of it--my nipples were on Red Alert, and every kiss, lick, and touch that Jaxon laid on my tender breasts was amplified.

I felt Jaxon's hand move between my legs, felt him touching me there. His fingertips slid down my cleft, dipping in a bit. My hips moved, pressing my body against him. He held up his fingers, then licked them.

"You're wet," he said. "Naughty little slut."

So many thoughts and emotions arose when he said that. There were all the appropriate thoughts, ranging from "of course I'm wet- YOU did this to me, you pervert!", to "I'm not a slut! I've only been with a few guys."

There were the guilty thoughts, the feelings of shame. There was the part of me that had been taught since I was a little girl to be ashamed of my sex, that it was a dirty thing to hide away and to never think about.

That part of me felt guilty for what Jaxon was doing to me, and for enjoying it. That part agreed that yes, I was naughty, that yes, I was a slut. That part of me was why my face flushed as red as my nipples, turning me scarlet with shame.

Finally, there was another part of me that reacted, a part of my psyche that I had never met before. This part of me reacted with pride, because it meant that Jaxon believed that I could even be a slut if I wanted to, that I was attractive enough for lots of men to want me that way. It meant that he wasn't looking at me as straight-laced Anastasia Munn, but a sex object. I didn't really want to be a sex object, but it was flattering to feel like I had the option.

The comment was so far off-base, so not "me", that I felt something waking up inside of me as a result. It was as if by calling me something that I was not, he was also giving me permission to be that something. By calling me a slut, he was giving permission for a secret inner slut to come out, to take control.

From any other guy, I would have been insulted. I would have called it quits, said the safe word, and been glad to never have anything to do with him again. From Jaxon, it seemed more like an encouraging compliment than anything else. Something changed in me.

"Yes, Master." I was almost purring.

"You like me touching you here, don't you?" His hand moved back between my legs, his fingers exploring the wet folds of my sex.

"Yes, Master." I did like it. There was an electric tingle as he brushed over my clitoris, a little pulse of pleasure. I let out a short sigh of breath.

"You like me touching your pussy." It was a statement, not a question. "Say it."

I didn't know what he meant at first. Hadn't I just told him that I liked it? Then I realized what he was going for, why he had used that word. He wanted me to say it.

I wasn't comfortable with that word. It was so raw, so explicit, so vulgar. But since I was handcuffed to a bed, naked, my legs spreading to provide Jaxon with easier access, maybe vulgar was only appropriate.

"I like you touching my… pussy, Master." When I said the word, I felt a small rush of heat down below, as if my body wanted to show me that it knew what I was talking about.

"Very good!" He was pleased. "And you liked sucking on my cock earlier."

I knew the game now. I blushed a little bit more, if that was possible. "I liked sucking on your cock, Master."

Another word that I was uncomfortable with. When I said it, though, I remembered what it was like to have him in my mouth. I remembered the feel, the taste. I wanted to experience that again.

"Oh, you'd like to do that again, would you?" Jaxon's words leapt out through a broad grin.

I didn't know what he was talking about at first. Had he read my mind? Then I realized that my head had moved toward him, had moved toward his crotch. My body had betrayed my desires. I licked my lips. I could make out the shape of him through the thin fabric of his pants.

"Yes, Master. I would love to suck your cock again."

"Since you've been good, I'll let you." He took his hand away from… away from my pussy. He unzipped his fly. He pulled out his… his cock. Somehow, that word was now the most appetizing way to describe the beautiful piece of flesh that I was looking at.

He moved onto the bed, straddling my chest. He put his hardening cock between my breasts, pushed them together until he was surrounded by my flesh. I could feel the heat from him, feel him hardening. He pinched my nipples, and I let out a strange sound of pleasure and of pain.

He put his hand on the back of my head. He repositioned himself. He told me, "I'm going to fuck your mouth."

I opened wide, and he filled it with his cock. I felt like it belonged, like I was more complete than I had been a moment ago. I sucked on him, eager to show him how much I enjoyed this, how much I enjoyed him. I wanted to use my hands to stroke him, but I was still cuffed to the bed.

Jaxon did most of the work. Just as he had said, he was fucking my mouth. I moved my head to match his rhythms, and I used my tongue to caress his shaft, but in this position he still had to do most of the movement. He didn't seem to mind.

It was frustrating not being able to use my hands. I wanted to touch him, but I couldn't. At the same time, the inability to use my hands meant freedom from expectation in that regard. I didn't have to worry about doing the wrong thing with my hands, or doing the right thing the wrong way, because I couldn't do anything at all.

We fell into an easy rhythm, his hand guiding my head, helping it move without forcing it to move. His cock slid in and out of my mouth, through my lips and over my tongue, again, and again, and again. I could hear his breathing speeding up. I could feel from the tempo of his thrusts that he was getting more excited.

"I'm going to go deeper. Remember to breathe through your nose," he said. Then he thrust deeper, holding my head in place. I didn't struggle. I was glad that he had warned me. I remembered to breathe through my nose.

He was deep in my mouth, with the end of his cock touching the back of my throat, threatening to make me gag. I wanted him deeper, but I didn't want to choke. I could feel him pulsing in my mouth with a slow and steady throb, throb, throb.

I held off as long as I could, but I gagged a bit. He held me there a fraction of a second longer, then pulled out. I coughed.

"Good," he said. He sounded pleased. "Very good. You're learning so much, so quickly."

Jaxon stood next to the bed, his erection bobbing tantalizingly over me. My jaw was sore, but I wanted more. I liked pleasing him, and I liked the intimacy of having him in my mouth.

He undid the cuffs, freeing my arms. In spite of the padding, my wrists were sore from where the cuffs had dug into my flesh. I rubbed them absentmindedly.

I coughed again. Without thinking, I tried to grab his hip with my hand, to steady myself. Except it wasn't his hip that I ended up grabbing. He stiffened.

I finished clearing my throat as I stroked my hand up and down his length. He let out a low groan. It was a sexy sound, almost primal.

I put my hand under his shirt and ran it up over the hard muscles of his stomach. His body was amazing, and the feel of his flesh made me want to see more of it. I tugged the bottom of his shirt out of his pants, then started working on the buttons. Soon the front of his shirt was open, his incredible chest and abs exposed to my sight as well as to my hands.

I couldn't help myself. I ran my tongue up his body, drawing a line from just below his navel, along his wonderful skin, until I reached his right nipple.

I took his nipple in my teeth, very gently nipping at it, then turning the nip into a kiss, followed by a few luxurious licks. I could feel it harden in my mouth.

I realized that he was letting me be the aggressor for a change, and I wondered just how far I could push it. I reached my hand up to cup his cheek, nervous that he might at any moment choose to punish me for my forwardness.

I kissed him softly, my tongue darting into his mouth for a taste. Our bodies were pushed closer together as we kissed, and I could feel his erection straining against my stomach. I loved the way that it felt, the physical feel of him as well as the emotions that surged within me, just from knowing that he wanted me.

I felt a warm liquid tingling down below, and little jolts of pleasure that made me shudder slightly. With my other hand, I reached down and started to stroke him again. He was huge, hard, and ready for me. I pulled away from his face so that I could look down, so that I could see my hand delicately wrapped around his girth.

He ran a finger down the side of my face, from my hairline to my jaw, tracing along my cheekbone. I gazed up at him, losing myself in his beautiful blue eyes. He ran his fingers gently over my lips and then pressed his mouth to mine.

He kissed me passionately while I slowly stroked him, feeling the soft outer skin sliding back and forth over his solid shaft. I felt like his eyes were staring into me, judging me. It was as if he was deciding how sincere I was being in my attentions. I wasn't sure what exactly he was looking for, but his mouth turned into a grin.

"You seem to enjoy touching my cock, don't you?" He seemed to be asking the question honestly, almost as if he was surprised by my lust.

"Yes, Master," I answered openly. On impulse, I spoke my mind. "I enjoy touching your cock. May I kiss it some more?"

He didn't answer me, but his grin broadened ever so slightly. He guided my head gently downward, letting me have my way. I took his head into my mouth, sucking on him. It was so good to have him back inside of me. It felt right. I felt at peace.

I widened my mouth even more, taking as much of his shaft into my mouth as I could. I loved the feel of his skin sliding over my tongue. I hit that point again where he was at the back of my mouth, teasing my throat.

This time, I was more prepared. I only gagged a very little, saliva seeping into my mouth as my body prepared to lubricate the foreign object enough to swallow it. I wasn't up for that trick just yet, though. I slowly pulled my head back, my lips clinging to his shaft, my tongue caressing it a temporary farewell.

Once he was out of my mouth, I licked my lips, cleared my throat a bit, then just licked up and down the sides of his cock. I noticed that I had been calling it that more often--his "cock" instead of some more sanitized euphemism. I'd been thinking it more, just like I'd been saying it more.

I was starting to really enjoy the way the word felt in my mouth. It was vulgar, but in a good way, a sexy way. It was one of those things that my mother had always tried to protect me from. "Don't say that; it's naughty!" she'd tell me.

It occurred to me that whenever parents teach their daughters that sex is naughty, they're also teaching them that naughty is sexy. The naughtiness of the word was part of the attraction.

Also, it was a good word, a strong word. Hard at the beginning, hard at the end, and nothing but "Oh!" in between.

"Your cock…" I realized that I had murmured that aloud, my mental musings turning into adoring vocalizations. My cheeks turned red. I hoped that he hadn't heard.

I leaned forward, wanting to taste it again. This time, instead of taking him inside of my mouth, I just held him in my hand and I licked him again, long caressing strokes from base to tip. His breathing was getting heavier. I knew that meant he liked it.

Jaxon shucked his shirt to the floor. He unbuttoned his pants while I stroked and licked his shaft, and pretty soon he was naked.

I tilted my head back so I could look up at him. He was looking down at me. Our eyes made contact, and I opened my mouth wide. I wanted him to see me, to be looking into my eyes--looking into my soul--as I showed him how much I wanted him.

I wanted him looking into me as my lips cover the head of his cock. I wanted him to know how grateful I was that he was letting me do this. I felt completely open to him, utterly vulnerable. I shed every form of armor and self-defense that my ego normally provided me, and I let him see in my eyes how I truly felt about him.

His own eyes widened as I took him into my mouth again. He broke contact first, closing his eyes as a guttural groan broke free from his mouth. The sound filled the silence between us, his unwilling admission of how he felt about me. Or, at least, how he felt about what I was doing to him.

As I slowly slid my lips further along his shaft, I slid my hand between his legs, caressing the shaven sac that held his testicles. I cupped it in my hand, fondling it gently. He had seemed to enjoy it before, and from the change in his breathing I assumed he was enjoying it again. I certainly was.

There was something entrancing about his body, about every part of him. I reveled in my exploration, in the sensation of his every curve and crevice.

I pulled back, stopping only when the swollen head of his cock was just about to pop out of my mouth, then took him all the way in again, swirling my tongue around his length. His eyes were still closed, his head tilted slightly back. His breath was coming in slow pants.

My mouth formed a smile around his cock. I liked knowing that I had that effect on him. My left hand grabbed him tightly around the base of his shaft while the other continued to play with his balls. He grunted. His cock began to twitch. He was thrusting his hips forward to meet me, sliding his length into my mouth as I slid forward to take him in. My smile turned into a soft moan of arousal, muffled by his flesh.

Suddenly, I felt his hand on the back of my head, fingers gripping my hair. He pulled my head back, sliding his cock out of my mouth. Then he was grabbing me under my arms, jerking me to my feet. I was hoisted into the air entirely as he tossed me up just enough to catch me again, this time with his hands cupped under my buttocks.

I yelped with surprise, my legs wrapping around his waist, my arms clinging to his shoulders. My mind was a step or two behind his actions. By the time I had adjusted to the fact that he had just picked me up, that my breasts were pressed against his sturdy pecs, and that I was suddenly looking at his face instead of his cock, Jaxon was lifting me even further upward, just a few inches, and was moving his waist. By the time my mind had realized that he was picking me up higher than he needed to just to throw me back on the bed, or to carry me somewhere else, I could feel the head of his cock prodding at my entrance. Then he was slamming me downward, smoothly penetrating me. He filled every inch of me.

Air escaped my lungs in a breathy cry of surprise and joy. Jaxon Kent was really inside of me, finally. All my fantasies for the past couple of years were suddenly made real. I felt a jolt of pleasure so sharp and so strong that for a moment I thought that I was coming, but then the jolt turned into a strong, steady current of pleasure instead of the crashing wave of orgasm.

He felt incredible inside of me. He was big, big enough that he stretched me out completely. My body tightly clung to him. I could feel the ridge of his cock deep inside of me. Jaxon just held me there for a moment, watching my face, which was good because I needed that time for my body to adjust to his size.

Jaxon lifted me up several inches, then let gravity pull me slowly down onto him again, making me feel wondrously impaled. That was when my mind fully caught up to the situation, and I found myself thinking, "Holy crap! We're having sex standing up. How strong is he?"

I didn't have time to dwell on that thought, because Jaxon was lifting me up again, then letting me slide back down. The next time he lifted me up, I used my legs to help him. Every time I slid down, he entered me to the hilt, my clitoris coming to rest against his pubic bone. When this happened, I started moving my hips, grinding myself more firmly against him.

I'd had no idea that sex like this could actually happen. I'd had no idea that it could be like this, that it could feel so good. If I had known, I would have tried it more often. I had never imagined. Suddenly, I fully understood what the big deal was about.

I realized that I was moaning aloud, making deep noises from within my chest. He kept penetrating me so fully that it felt like air was being pushed right out of my lungs. I felt like he was controlling my body; I felt possessed.

"Good God!" His words were a passionate groan. "You are so fucking tight."

I didn't respond. I was embarrassed. I was flattered. I was blushing.

Jaxon continued to lift me up, then slide me back down on his cock, again and again. His strength was amazing. Feeling the power of his muscles and seeing them strain underneath his skin was such a turn-on. He was starting to sweat--or we both were--and our chests slickly glided over each other. My nipples, still on red alert from the clothespins, sent little shockwaves of pain and pleasure as they rubbed up against the solid muscles of his torso.

The sensations all started to blend together. The pleasure from his cock. The stretching sensation in my pussy. The controlled grind of my clitoris on his pubic bone. The pain in my nipples. The pleasure in my nipples. The soreness of my own muscles. The feel of his muscles underneath my hands and between my thighs.

His sounds. My sounds. Our sounds.

My breath quickened, as he pumped in and out of me. I realized that I was on the verge, about to climax. I remembered that I wasn't supposed to do that without permission. Part of me wanted to just go on and do it, to unleash the explosion that was building inside of me. The other part of me remembered the level of punishment that Jaxon could dish out when he chose.

I closed my eyes, doing my best to hold off my impending orgasm, but as much as I fought against it, each stroke of his cock inside of me brought me closer and closer to going over the brink into forbidden ecstasy.

"You like me fucking you." He liked me to affirm the obvious.

"Yes, Master." Talking was difficult. It was distracting, but somehow still put me even closer to that edge.

"You want to come for me, don't you?"

He no doubt could tell how close I was. My body desperately clutched at him, frantic for the impending pleasure, but fearful of the pain if I disappointed him.

"God," I managed to gasp between thrusts. Moisture ran down my cheek. I couldn't tell if it was a tear or a bead of sweat. "Yes, Master, yes!"

"Hold it. Don't come until I command it."

His own breath was deeper and faster. He was close to orgasm as well. Was he going to punish me now? Was he going to come inside of me, then leave me unfulfilled, cuffed to the bed?

The up-and-down slide continued, the exquisite sensation torturing me. I was about to come. I had to stop it. My mind rapidly searched for any ounce of sensation that wasn't pleasure, any thought or feeling that wouldn't release that building pressure into an explosion of bliss.

My mind found the pain, the ache in my nipples as they brushed against his body. I pressed myself even more firmly up against him, my rock-hard nipples dragging roughly across his chest. It stung, and I focused on the stinging. I focused on the pain, tried to find shelter in it, tried to find protection from the raging storm of pleasure that was threatening to sweep me away.

It worked, barely, and I was able to hold back the explosion. The back of my mind was lost in the bliss of sex, but the front of my mind was determined to distract itself with the pain in my breasts. I was dimly aware of Jaxon's breaths getting even faster, even closer together.

"Now," he said.

I didn't even have time to thank God; I just quit holding on to the pain, and let myself get swept away.

Somebody was crying out, somebody was screaming. I think it was both of us. I could feel his cock swell inside of me, feel his body explode it contents into my flesh, but most of the details of Jaxon's orgasm were lost, overwhelmed like fireworks in a thunderstorm, as my own orgasm roared over me.

The sheer force of the pleasure left me shuddering, mindless, unable to breathe. I held on to his body tightly, as if I was holding on for dear life. He held me securely in place, until the only motion in our bodies was in our hips, until even that movement slowed, then ceased. He stood there, holding me, his cock still pulsing and throbbing inside of me.

He was shaking now, his muscle no longer able to hold us both up. He made eye contact with me, grinned that grin, then turned and fell forward onto the bed, landing on top of me as my back made contact with the soft mattress.

The weight of him pushed a sigh out of my lungs, a sigh that turned into a moan as the momentum of our bodies pushed his cock even deeper inside of me, as his body rubbed up against my clit again. I shuddered a final time, either in a large aftershock or in a new, smaller orgasm, it was hard to tell.

We just lay there, exhausted, with him still on top of me. He kissed my breasts, then gave each of them a slightly stinging slap. I was too exhausted to care. He'd been doing most of the work during sex, but I'd still been using muscles that I didn't even know that I had, just to help us stay upright.

Jaxon shifted position so that his weight wasn't on me as much, put his head on the pillow, and looked at me with those blue eyes of his. He was judging me again, analyzing me. From the smile, it seemed that he was pleased.

After a time, his eyes closed. I think he went to sleep. I closed my own eyes and just rested for a while.

It was the first time that I'd really had just to think since this whole thing started, since I ran into Jaxon at the bar. I had a lot to think about, and I had a lot of emotions to sort through.

Lying there with Jaxon on top of me, still inside of me, I mostly felt happy. I felt complete, and satisfied. "Completely satisfied," I thought to myself, and mentally giggled.

It was just so wonderful being with him this way. The sex was fantastic, and the afterglow was just as good. There was something so secure, so safe in being with him--at least when he wasn't inflicting pain on me.

Actually, I realized, I mostly felt safe and secure even when he was hurting me. I trusted him. When I thought about that, it was something that was really rare. I wouldn't have trusted any of my previous boyfriends to do that sort of thing, to paddle me and such. Not just because I wasn't into the pain, but because I wasn't sure of their competence.

With Jaxon, I never doubted his ability to inflict exactly as much pain as he wanted to: no more, no less. The guys I'd been with before? They couldn't even dance without stepping on my toes. I didn't think that Jaxon would ever hurt me accidentally.

I let those thoughts lay there in my brain a bit, let them sink in. I realized that I'd just compared Jaxon to "my *other* boyfriends," and I felt naive. Jaxon wasn't my boyfriend. I didn't know what this was exactly, but it wasn't holding hands on the beach, and it wasn't going to last. It couldn't. It was based on a lie that was going to come out sooner or later.

Yet again, I wondered what the hell I was doing here, what weird twist in my brain had given me the impulse to pass myself off as a Mayflower. With that single lie, I had fallen into a new world of both heavens and hells.

Even if I made it through this weekend, what next? I go back to my normal life? Jaxon and I go right back to normal, with me running occasional errands for him at the office? We go back to idle flirting and chit-chat on Friday nights?

I felt a small stab in my heart, felt my arms hold Jaxon more tightly, as if I could physically keep him with me for the long haul. I knew better, though. Whatever happened on Monday, Jaxon only kept his girls for a weekend. Then he was done with them. Then he'd be done with me.

I felt foolish and I felt used. It didn't seem right for Jaxon to do that, to have his way with girl after girl, weekend after weekend. It didn't seem right for him to use them that way, for him to use *me* that way.

Then again, I was using him to fulfil my own fantasy. I'd conned my way in here. I'd known ahead of time that this wasn't going to be real, wasn't going to last. I'd done it anyway, I guess because part of me felt like it would be worth it. Part of me felt like it was better to be used by Jaxon for a weekend than to never be with him at all.

I felt like I should have more pride than that, but as I searched through my emotions, I realized that I didn't. Even though I was starting to think that life would be unbearable after the weekend was over, I didn't really feel bad about trading my future happiness for one weekend with this man, deranged as the weekend was turning out to be.

I opened my eyes and looked at his nude body. He was like a perfect sculpture, like a god. It was a shock seeing him there, so naked, so flawless, even though I already knew he was there. I looked at him, trying to drink in every detail, trying to memorize every part of him so that I'd have something to think back on when all this was over.

I started to tear up. The situation was so fucked-up, but I really didn't want to lose him, and I knew that I was going to. I didn't know how I could face him again at work after this, how things could ever go back to normal. Then again, when he found out what I'd done, I'd probably lose my job anyway.

Then I started to itch. Jaxon had come inside of me, and his penis was still inside of me, and something about that combo really started to become uncomfortable, itchy.

He looked so wonderful, just lying there asleep, that I didn't want to wake him. I tried moving my hips a bit, adjusting things. It didn't help. I tried moving my internal muscles a bit, tried to re-arrange things there. Jaxon started to get hard.

The next time I tried to move my hips, Jaxon's hips moved a bit too. He got even harder. It actually helped with the itching, made it less severe. Then he fully hardened, and it started to feel good.

Pretty soon, we were both moving our hips, pushing our bodies slowly together, then slightly apart again. Jaxon opened his eyes, looked at me. He grinned that grin.

He moved his body more fully on top of my own, his weight pushing me into the mattress. He kissed me, my mind melting a bit as his tongue slipped into my mouth. I didn't notice that he took hold of my wrists until he had stretched my arms out over my head. I only realized what he was doing in the moment before the cuffs clicked into place.

The moment my hands were trapped, I wanted to use them. I wanted to reach out and touch him. I wanted to feel his hard muscles underneath my hands, to explore his body. I reached out my hands and was rewarded with a metallic "clack" sound as my bonds held me back. I groaned in frustration.

Jaxon's cock somehow seemed to grow even harder inside of me, feeling like an iron bar pinning me in place. A bar that was slowly moving, impaling me repeatedly, at a torturous pace. I moved my hips, trying to increase the speed of my penetration, but Jaxon moved his hips along with me, negating my efforts.

He took his time. My body had time to dwell on each centimeter of his cock sliding in and out of me. He supported himself with one hand, using his other hand to explore my body with gentle, teasing caresses.

He stroked my cheeks, my ears, my neck. His hands moved over my shoulders, arms, and breasts. His fingers danced along my flesh, teasing me to the height of arousal until I wanted to beg him to just take me, to fuck me hard until I came.

He changed positions, lifting my hips until he could shift his weight to his knees, freeing his other arm. Then he took a breast in each hand, squeezing them, his fingertips pinching my tender nipples.

I took in a sharp breath through my nose. The sensation was intense, a mixture of pleasure and pain. He soothed the pain with his mouth, enhancing the pleasure by sucking gently, and by light licks of his tongue.

When I started to squirm, he gave each of my breasts a light, playful slap. My breasts bounced, but it didn't hurt or anything. Then he slapped them again, harder. He was hitting the soft parts of my flesh, avoiding the nipples, but my nipples were so sensitive that they gave a little cry of sensation.

There was more sting than outright pain, and there was even a little spark of pleasure. Also, I liked the feel of his hand on my flesh, of the bounce in my breasts after the impact. He slowly increased the force behind the slaps, and it started to sting regularly, but I was still so turned on that it didn't matter. The skin of my breasts started to blush from his attentions.

He nodded at the reddish-pink hue of my flesh, then he caressed his way down my body until his hands were on my hips, holding me in place as he thrust in and out of me. His speed increased, creating pools of pleasure in my lower regions, in my pussy.

I let out a contented sigh. My breasts still burned a bit from the slapping, but the the pain was all but washed away in the sensations of sex. Most of what I felt was a warmth, and a mild ache. It felt almost satisfying, like the burn after a good workout.

My hips tried to move with him, to push up to meet his thrusts, but he held me firmly in his hands. He was in control.

He moved his hands from my hips, up along the backs of my thighs, and my body practically sang under his touch. Everywhere his hands touched me, my flesh came alive and wanted more.

His hands caught me under my knees, pulling me up, pushing my legs toward my chest. That changed the angle of penetration, and even though he stopped going in all the way, I felt somehow more satisfied, more filled from each thrust.

With this new angle, though, his body was no longer pushing up against my clit. My pussy was stretched wide by him, my clit exposed, vulnerable, and unsatisfied. Jaxon looked down, watching where our bodies were joined, watching himself slip in and out of me. I had never had a man do that before, had a man just watch our bodies merging.

I blushed, feeling exposed. I could also feel my body getting wetter, more aroused. I found my legs spreading a bit wider to enhance his view.

The pleasure kept pooling inside of me, kept building up. I found myself squirming, moving my hips with his rhythm now that he had released them. I found myself straining at the cuffs, trying to touch him, or maybe to touch myself. My clitoris was swollen with lust, crying out for attention.

Jaxon moved his hands to my ankles, holding them up, pinning them together, pulling my butt up off of the bed. He gripped them with his left hand, freeing his right hand for something else.

I should have expected what happened next, but I didn't. The loud smack of his hand on my flesh startled me, and I gave out a yelp of surprise. Then the nerves in my buttocks caught up to the sound, carrying the pain to my brain, and I yelped again. It wasn't that the pain was that bad, just that it was a surprise.

Jaxon spanked me again, on the other cheek. The angle wasn't very good, so the impact wasn't as hard. Then he struck me again, on the back of my thigh, then the other thigh. His hand struck a steady beat on the softer parts of my flesh, slapping and spanking me again and again, from my thighs to my buttocks, then back to my thighs again.

My body futilely prepared to defend itself. Adrenaline and other hormones surged through me. My skin burned from his assault--I could feel it blushing. My body was on red alert, and every sensation was amplified.

That's when Jaxon licked his thumb and moved it onto my clit.

The change in sensation caught me completely off-guard. My poor little bud was already torturously aroused, already straining for any stimulation that it could get, and the spanking had heightened my senses so much that when Jaxon touched me there, I screamed.

Almost immediately, I screamed again as Jaxon's thumb rubbed me to orgasm.

I hadn't realized how close I was until it happened, hadn't noticed how much pleasure and pressure had been slowly stoked inside of me until it reached a boiling point, until I exploded into a mass of screaming, thrashing ecstasy.

The pleasure splashed up through my body, starting in my clit and my pussy, then gushed up my spine, drowning my mind in a whirlpool. I gasped for air. I pulled against the cuffs, making useless metallic noises as my arms futilely fought to get free.

I kicked my legs and Jaxon released them, then trapped them again, this time using his arms to trap the backs of my knees as he shifted position until his weight was back on his arms and he was able to fully penetrate me again.

My orgasm was still rippling through me as Jaxon started thrusting into me, sheathing his entire length in my body. Each time he hilted himself in me, there was a slight pause. There was a fraction of a beat where his body was pushed up against my clit, and he just held it there, just long enough to push the sensation home before he pulled away again.

"My slave," Jaxon's voice was stern, commanding. "I didn't give you permission to come. You'll have to do it again, this time when I tell you to."

Was he serious? Again? I was still coming from a moment ago, little waves flowing through my body, my mind only barely able to swim to the surface, and he wanted me to do it again?

He was serious. He kept up that rhythm, that tormentous beat of his body against mine. He kept plunging into me, kept finding sweet spots within me, kept forcing pleasure into me until I couldn't take it anymore.

"Please!" I begged. "I can't take it. Please, may I come? Please let me!"

Jaxon didn't answer immediately, as if he was considering the option. His body kept moving. I squirmed and writhed beneath him, fighting against the overwhelming sensations that he was inflicting upon me. His breathing grew deeper, faster, as he watched my desperation. Finally, he answered.

"Yes, slave. You may come."

I did, and it was just as fierce as before. I lost myself in that whirlpool of pleasure, my mind only dimly aware of Jaxon crying out, of a warm splash within me as he joined me in bliss.

# CHAPTER 13

We showered again. We needed to. Once again Jaxon soaped me up and scrubbed me clean. He took care of me as if I was a prize of some kind. It made me feel a bit insulted as if I was a pet, but it also made me feel special--important and wanted.

As we stood there under the spray, Jaxon reached between my legs, petting me there.

"We're going to have to do something about this, I think," he said.

I didn't have permission to speak, so I looked at him quizzically. Hadn't we just done something about that? Like, twice in a row?

"The hair. We should shave it." His hand continued to pet me there.

Oh. I was a bit embarrassed, and a bit insulted. He could see it in my face.

"What is it, slave?" He seemed slightly irritated. "You may speak."

"Shave it all? Why, Master? What's wrong with it as it is?"

"Nothing's wrong with it, slave." He seemed amused. "I just prefer my women to be completely bare down there."

I didn't know what to say. Jaxon shut off the water and I was content to let the matter drop, since it seemed like he didn't want me to shave right away. Maybe it was an idle fancy, and he'd forget about it.

After the shower, he dried me off with a large towel and led me through the penthouse, to a small room off to the side of the main living room area. When he opened the door, I noticed that this room seemed warmer than the cool air of the rest of the apartment. Then I saw why.

The floor, walls, and high ceiling of this room were all covered in ceramic tiles, patterns of blue, yellow, and white. The far wall was covered in windows, though it was hard to see out past the shelves of green plants that had been placed there to soak up the sunlight. On two of the walls, there were plain wooden benches. On the remaining wall, there was a row of hooks with towels and bathrobes hanging from them.

In the center of the room was a massive hot tub.

"You will relax here while I prepare some food." He pulled the cover off of the tub as he spoke, the thick, insulated pad folding up in the middle so that it could be pushed off to the side, out of the way. "You will stay here until I return. There is a bathroom through that door. You may use it if necessary. If you wander any place other than this room or the bathroom, the transgression will be added to your punishment book."

I nodded, then added a verbal, "Yes, Master."

He left, and I approached the tub. I'd been in a hot tub before, but not all that often. I considered it to be a rare luxury, and I couldn't help but smile as I looked over the controls. I turned on all the jets--on low--and I climbed on in.

The water was so hot that it burned at first, as I was sticking my legs in, but I stood there for a few moments until my body adjusted, then submerged more and more of my body, adjusting at each step, until I was able to sink into one of the built-in seats.

I could feel the jets working on my back, massaging my tired muscles. The heat sank into me, soothing my various aches and pains, and I let out a contented sigh.

As I relaxed, my body grew limper and my legs spread out a bit, and suddenly a jet that had been focused on my knees was hitting my crotch instead. It was the large, central jet, and it was far enough away for the force to be rather diffuse, but it still caught me off-guard with the erotic sensations of the water softly pummeling my private bits.

I realized that I'd never been naked in a hot tub before. Most of the times I'd been in one had been with my mom, when we were in a hotel on the way to visit family. I'd never been in a private tub before, and the ability to be naked in the water felt decadent and freeing.

I felt some pleasant tingling between my legs, and I moved to a different seat. That sort of thing might be interesting another time, but right now I needed to relax more than anything else. My private parts were already being well taken care of this weekend.

I smiled drowsily as I thought of all the sex I'd been having. My eyes closed, and I had tiny, dream-like flashbacks of sex, and orgasms, and Jaxon, and spankings, and Jaxon again, and again. Jaxon. I couldn't believe that I was here, doing these things with him. I couldn't believe that he'd been doing these things to me.

Part of my brain once again tried reminding me that it was all coming to an end. I probably had less than thirty-six hours left with the man before it all came to ruin. I shut that part of my brain down and focused on the good parts, on the rainbows that were somehow here before the storm.

I might have dozed a little, or I might have simply been so relaxed that I lost track of what I was thinking. My mind wandered from one thing to the other, my thoughts became strange and dreamlike. At one point I had the thought that cubicles were their own kind of bondage. At another point, I pictured my mom holding a whip, telling me that I was her slave. If I didn't take care of her, she'd die, and it would go in my punishment book.

Then Jaxon was there, his hand stroking my hair, gently waking me. He helped me out of the tub. He pulled a large, unbelievably fluffy towel off of a hook, and he dried me off thoroughly. Then he led me to the kitchen and sat me across from him at a small table.

On the table was our lunch, which turned out to be a hearty salad, with kale, bacon, slices of hard-boiled egg, cherry tomatoes, and some kind of delicious white shredded cheese. I was kind of surprised and relieved that it wasn't something fancier.

I was half expecting lobster, or some weird food that I wasn't familiar with. I was glad to see something normal and palatable. I realized that I was famished, so I sat down and prepared to dig in.

Then I caught myself, and I waited to see what Jaxon would do. Maybe I wasn't supposed to eat until he ate, or maybe we were supposed to say grace or something. He simply nodded, lifted his fork, and started eating.

We ate in silence for a while. Then, surprisingly, Jaxon struck up a conversation. We'd talked often in the bar, but he hadn't been very chatty this weekend, and I wasn't allowed to speak without permission.

"Slave," Jaxon said, "why don't you like the idea of having your pussy completely shaved?"

I wasn't quite sure how to answer. "I just don't really get it, Master. I think it'd make me look like a little girl down there."

Jaxon considered the statement before answering. "Perhaps. I can't really say, because I've never seen what a little girl looks like down there. I hadn't ever really considered that aspect of it before. For me, the pleasure is simply in seeing more of you. There are other factors, like less chance of a stray hair getting in my mouth when I lick you, but overall I just feel like a woman is more naked when she's removed of hair, more vulnerable."

I didn't know what to say, so I just nodded.

"When you shave your legs and your armpits, does that make you feel like a little girl?"

I thought about it. "No, Master. It makes me feel… attractive. I feel sexier with shaved legs."

He nodded, taking a drink from his glass of water. I had my own but hadn't picked it up yet. After the hot tub, plain water was exactly what I needed, but I'd been expecting something else. Wine, perhaps.

"I have decided that you may keep your hair, if you wish. Although I think you would look so much better without it. I'd like to see you completely." He glanced downward as he said it, as if he could see right through the table, as if he was looking at me with x-ray eyes. "Still, I only have you for the weekend. For such a short time, it probably doesn't matter."

"Thank you, Master."

I was glad that he was willing to let the matter drop. Somehow, though, I was a bit disappointed. Now that he'd brought it up, I was curious what I'd look like, what I'd feel like, completely shaved down there. I think that part of me was hoping that he'd force the issue, that he'd make me submit to him.

"That brings us to another subject."

He was still authoritative, but there was something off about his voice. He was too calm, too careful, as if he was on guard about something.

"If I was to propose to you that we sign an additional contract, one that kept you here during the week, extending your stay until Friday night, would that be of interest to you?"

I didn't know what to say. I was shocked. I'd been bracing myself for all this to end Sunday night, or Monday morning at the latest. I leapt on his question, eager to stave off the upcoming disaster. "Oh, yes, Master! I'd like to stay."

Again he nodded. Again he seemed carefully guarded. "Have you enjoyed your time here, then?"

I wasn't sure how to answer that. Some of it was wonderful, but some of it was horrible.

"I've learned a lot during my stay, Master," I said. I tried to be honest without being offensive. "It has been the most intense experience of my life."

He kept nodding, looking thoughtful. "Good. I will consider drawing up a weekday contract, then. If your company continues to be as pleasant as it has been, I think that we could both benefit from the additional time together."

There was silence for a few moments while we continued our meal. Jaxon broke the silence. "I don't normally do weekday contracts."

My mouth was full, so I simply nodded. I didn't really know what to say to that anyway. All I knew was that I might have more time with Jaxon, and I was happy about that. Although that also meant more punishments. What if he decided to crank things up a notch? What if he decided to use the cane? I realized that perhaps I had been too quick to answer him.

"In fact," he continued, "I've already broken a few of my personal rules for you."

"You have?" I blurted out. I'd assumed that everything we were doing was business as normal on his end of things. "Like what?"

Jaxon glared at me, and I added a belated "Master."

"You slip up on that one too often." He pointed his fork at me as he said this. "You're going to feel it tonight. If I didn't know better, I'd start to think that you were misbehaving on purpose, just to make things rougher on yourself."

"Oh, no, Master!" I felt like offering an explanation or an apology, but the only things that sprang to mind were things that would blow my cover. I didn't want him to know how new I was to this, how far in over my head I was. I didn't want him to send me home, not like that.

I let my statement hang there, hoping that it didn't sound like I was playing coy.

"You resisted when I put the leash on you." Jaxon sounded both analytical and chastising. "Are you too good to crawl, slave? Or was the collar not up to your standards in some way?"

Hell, yes, I was too good to crawl! I didn't think he'd like that answer, though. I didn't want to be punished for talking back, for standing up to him on this point. I tried to go the other route. "The collar…"

I trailed off. It suddenly felt like a trap. Was he trying to bait me into saying that I was too good for the collar? That seemed like a swift road toward punishment as well. I tried to think of what to say, how to get out of the bind that I was in. Painful seconds of silence ticked by. Then Jaxon spoke.

"It is an old collar, and it's been very well-used over the years. It occurs to me that it might have been too large around your slender neck. No matter. We can get you a new one."

"Thank you, Master." I didn't know what else to say. This felt like one of those gifts that can't be refused. Also, I was distracted by his comment about my neck being slender. Did that mean he thought I was pretty?

We finished the meal in relative silence. Jaxon asked me several more questions. Did the clothespins teach me the proper lesson? Was the shower to my liking? How were my bruises feeling? Did I find the hot tub soothing?

I answered honestly and briefly, remembering to call him "Master" each time. Yes, the clothespins taught me a valuable lesson. Yes, I loved the shower. I still had some aches and tender spots, but nothing serious. Yes, the hot tub was wonderful.

It was weird, making BDSM small-talk with Jaxon. On one hand, it felt comfortable to a point, kind of like our conversations in the bar. His eyes twinkled when he looked at me or when he made some kind of joke. There was that connection that I'd always felt between us.

On the other hand, I was sitting naked at his kitchen table, eating salad and being interrogated about a number of painful and humiliating things that he'd done to me, and I had to keep calling him "Master."

That last part just seemed unfair. I never had to call him "Boss" at work, but when we're off the clock, things get more formal? I smiled at the weirdness of it all, and because I had another flashback to "I Dream of Jeannie."

# CHAPTER 14

After lunch, Jaxon told me to go back to my room. I had exactly fifteen minutes to use the bathroom if I needed to, to dry my hair, and to pick out a nice coat and shoes to wear when we went shopping. The closet in the bedroom should have everything that I need. I took all this to be his strange way of letting me know that we were going shopping.

I asked about what other clothes he wanted me to wear-- remembering to call him "Master"--and he informed me that the coat and shoes would suffice. Which I supposed meant that I wasn't allowed any other clothing. Maybe we weren't going shopping after all?

Jaxon gave me a nod that seemed to say that I should hurry up, the clock was ticking, so I left without asking any more questions. I went back to the bedroom and saw the bed and the handcuffs, and remembered what we'd done there. I had a flashback of how it felt to be cuffed, to be helpless while Jaxon had his way with me. My cheeks flushed, and I felt a shiver of pleasure between my legs.

I hurried on to the bathroom, sat down and started to pee. I looked around for a hair dryer but didn't see one. I didn't want to ask Jaxon where one was, but I didn't think I'd have much choice. I was trying to figure out if I had enough time to search the bedroom for a dryer when Jaxon walked in.

I jumped. "What are you doing!?"

"I brought you a hair dryer." Jaxon smirked a little as he held it out to me. I was mortified. I was still mid-stream. I took the hair dryer, my cheeks turning red with emotions.

"Come, come," Jaxon chided me. "You have no secrets from me, slave. Don't be silly. And you forgot to call me 'Master' again. I'll go update your punishment book while you finish getting ready. Hurry up--we don't have any time for nonsense."

Then he left.

I finished peeing. I had never in my life had anybody stand in the bathroom talking to me while I was on the toilet before. The man had no concept of personal space.

Thank God I was only peeing!

After I was off the toilet, I dried my hair and brushed it with a brush I found in the cabinet behind the sink. Then I went to the closet in the bedroom.

It was a walk-in, of course, with rows of women's clothing on either wall, and a mirror at the far end. I got distracted browsing through some of the clothing. A lot of what I was looking at were essentially costumes.

There was a nurse's outfit, a nun's habit, several leather things that I couldn't identify, a policewoman's uniform... I smothered a laugh. Jaxon was one kinky bastard!

Not that the contents of the closet were my first clue.

I remembered that I was in a hurry and started to go to the end where I saw a collection of long women's coats, but something caught my eye. I saw a light blue blouse on a hanger. It looked familiar. I pulled it off to look at it and realized why. I had this exact same blouse at home.

I sifted through the section that had the normal clothing, the stuff that wasn't just costumes, and I realized that there was a large section that was composed of exact outfits that I had at home. What the hell?

A chill went through me as a thought occurred to me. Maybe I didn't have them at home. Maybe Jaxon had gone through my closet and brought a bunch of my clothing here, without my permission. Or perhaps he'd had his driver or another servant do it.

"Three minutes, slave!" Jaxon's voice rang out from the other room, making me jump guiltily as if I had been doing something wrong.

I didn't know what to make of this. I didn't know why he'd have a bunch of my clothing here, or what it could mean. I focused on getting a coat and some shoes.

I started with the shoes, and it turned out to be harder than I expected. Every piece of footwear had heels, even the boots, some of which were thigh high. I eventually found a nice pair of black Jimmy Choo shoes similar to a pair that I had at home, and I put them on.

By that time, I didn't have much time to pick out a coat so I just grabbed the first thing that looked like it would go past my knees, which turned out to be a beige and black Kate Spade oversized trench coat.

I pulled it on and made it out to the living room just in time to hear Jaxon counting down my remaining seconds.

"Seven… six… five…"

He heard my heels clicking on the floor. "Ah, there you are. Just in time. Shall we?"

He extended his arm and I took it, partially for balance. These shoes looked the same as the pair I had at home, but the balance was a bit different. Besides I didn't exactly wear my own pair very often. They looked good, but by the end of the day they felt horrible on my feet.

Jaxon whisked me out the door, past that replica of David in the front hall and into the elevator. On the way down, I realized that he was completely serious about taking me shopping and became painfully aware of how completely naked I was underneath my coat.

The big, black car waited for us out front.

# CHAPTER 15

The drive across town was mostly silent. I thought about asking where we were going, but I didn't feel like going through the rigmarole of getting permission, calling him master, and so forth.

Apparently we were going to get me a new collar. Beyond that I'd just have to wait and see, to trust Jaxon not to do anything really insane, like kicking me out of the car in a bad part of town.

I spent most of the drive hoping that I'd get some underwear, a shirt, and a skirt with my new collar.

I recognized the region of the city that we finally ended up in. It wasn't too far from where I lived, actually, although I'd never been to this specific area. I saw a shopping mall off in the distance, and I found a perverse anxiety growing inside of me, the notion that he intended to take me to a pet store in the mall, buy me a collar, then walk me out back to the car completely naked except for the collar and a leash.

We passed the mall, but the image of being paraded past dozens of mall-goers stuck with me. My heart was beating faster than normal.

We eventually pulled into the parking lot of a building I didn't recognize. It was unmarked, except for some graffiti. Somebody had spray-painted a rearing horse on the wall next to the door. A disembodied arm lashed out at the horse with a whip of black paint.

Once we were parked, Jaxon came around to open my door like a gentleman opening a carriage door for his lady. He extended his arm. I took it, and he walked me to the door. The driver stayed with the car.

Instead of trying the knob, Jaxon pushed a doorbell and looked up at a camera that was over the door. A moment later there was a buzzing sound. The door opened, and we walked inside.

Jaxon exchanged greetings with the doorman, as if they were longtime friends. Jaxon didn't introduce me and the man didn't acknowledge me, so I busied myself by reading a series of small signs on the wall just inside the entrance.

"We welcome all customers, no matter what you are wearing or not wearing."

"Adults Only: 18 or older."

"Any Persons Offended By Nudity or Adult Activities Should Turn Back Now."

The first sign made me smile and gave me a bit of relief. The second sign was no surprise--we were apparently at an adult-oriented sex shop or something.

The third sign made me wonder what exactly I was in for.

Jaxon and the doorman finished up their pleasantries, and Jaxon led me into the main room of the establishment. I'd never seen anything like it.

It was like a department store for kink. I saw rack after rack after rack of oddities: leather and rubber garments, peephole bras, crotchless panties, corsets, stockings, and countless unusual toys that I'd only glimpsed in the pages of an "Adam & Eve" catalog.

There was another section that looked like equestrian gear: whips, bridles, saddles, ropes, bits, riding crops, and other such stuff that wouldn't have been shocking except I knew that they weren't intended for horses.

"You haven't been here before," Jaxon observed. "Well, you may have a look around while I talk to Master Rolando."

I kind of wanted to stay near Jaxon. This place was so strange, and Jaxon was the only familiar thing within sight. Nonetheless, I nodded and said, "Yes, Master."

Then Jaxon strode toward the back of the store, and I was left alone. I turned to look around, and noticed that I was standing next to a display rack of dildos. Many were shaped like penises, many were not. They came in a wide variety of hues, ranging from various flesh tones to every color you might find in a Crayola box.

I saw a life-sized plastic forearm with a fist at the end, and tried to figure out what it was doing with the sex toys. Then I understood, and turned a bit red. People did that?

I scurried off to a section filled with clothing.

Really, it wasn't much better. There were anatomically correct mannequins displaying corsets and garters and other such impracticalities. I caught myself staring at one of them, amazed at the amount of detail that went into the plastic nipples that were poking out through decorative holes in its lace bra.

It was like there was an entire industry that I had absolutely no idea about. I mean I'd heard of sex toys. I'd flipped through a naughty catalog or two that somehow got sent to me by mail. A lot of this stuff, though, looked expensive, high-end.

The mannequins were so detailed that they could almost be mistaken for people. Hesitantly, I reached out and touched one on its bare leg. It didn't feel exactly like flesh, but it was soft, not like the hard plastic mannequins in other stores.

My eyes strayed to the mannequin's sculpted vulva, and I realized that it looked like it was designed for actual penetration. Then I saw a price tag hanging off of the mannequin, one that was attached to the leg itself. It was upward of seven thousand dollars, which seemed like way too much for the outfit that it was wearing.

That's when things clicked into place, and I realized that the price tag wasn't for the clothing, it was for the plastic woman herself. These weren't just mannequins--they were sex dolls.

I stepped back, my cheeks turning red from embarrassment over my naivety. I remembered Marianna talking about these things once: they'd been featured on some cable show she watched, a show about new trends in sex. How the hell did I end up in this store instead of her?

I took a few steps back, still looking at the mannequin. I was amazed at the detail. If I was far enough away that they looked almost exactly like real people, except that they weren't moving. I took another step back and felt something poke my back, felt my shoulder hit a torso, and saw a head above my shoulder out of the corner of my eye. I'd bumped into somebody.

I turned to say "excuse me," then stopped. It was just another mannequin: a male doll that was sporting a huge plastic erection. That's what had jabbed me in the back when I bumped into it.

I scurried away from the clothing section, even redder than I'd been when I went in.

I ended up in part of the store that was filled with paddles and other spanking paraphernalia. At this point, that was fine with me. It was better than bumping into some doll's penis while staring at another doll's breasts. It was better than standing in the dildo aisle.

There were all kinds of paddles there: wood paddles, plastic paddles, Ping-Pong paddles, a canoe paddle.... I stopped to browse the section with the leather paddles and found one that looked like the one that Jaxon had used on me.

I picked the paddle up and felt the weight of it in my hand. I swung it through the air a few times. It was heavy. It was hard to believe that I'd let him use something like this on me, but, then again, I still had the bruises.

I put the paddle back on its hook and turned around to look at the rack behind me. This one had a variety of whip-like instruments, except that there were a lot more than just one whip coming out of the handle. The phrase "cat o' nine tails" came to mind, except that most of them had far more than nine tails.

I found one that had dozens of rubber strings coming out of the handle. I swished it through the air a few times, then got curious. I whopped myself on the forearm with it once, then again, harder. It barely hurt. Granted, I hadn't put a lot of force behind it, but it also seemed like the rubber strands took some of the impact out.

I put that one back and grabbed a different one. This one had a bunch of leather cords for the tails. I whopped myself on the arm with it twice, and then stopped. That one stung. It wasn't too bad, though.

If you were expecting the pain, it didn't seem to hurt as much. I wondered if whipping yourself was kind of like tickling yourself, if the fact that I was testing these on my own arm meant that it hurt less than if somebody else had hit me with the same force.

I wandered out of that aisle and ended up face-to-behind with another mannequin. This one was up on a small raised platform that rose maybe a couple of feet off of the ground. The doll was bent over something that looked like a padded saw-horse with leather upholstery. Her ankles and wrists were hanging down next to the legs of the thing, and it was easy enough to picture the doll being tied or cuffed in that position.

I wondered if Jaxon had something like that in his penthouse somewhere, in one of the rooms I hadn't been in yet. I wondered what it would be like to be bound to it that way, my buttocks and private parts on display, my breasts hanging down accessibly to either side of the wooden body. I started to get a little bit turned on.

Since the doll's posterior happened to be positioned at almost my eye level, I couldn't help but check it out a bit. The level of detail was incredible. That first doll I had looked at had actually had fake pubic hair on it, but this one seemed to lack that feature.

Her fake vulva was partially shadowed between her legs, but it looked completely hairless. I bent my knees a bit to get a closer look. There wasn't any hair there at all. The doll didn't look like a little girl, though. Not one bit.

I wondered how many varieties these dolls came in, how customizable they were. Whoever had ordered this one must have liked improbably large breasts. On a whim, I smacked the doll on its exposed ass. The feeling was surprisingly realistic.

"Thank you," the doll said. "May I have another?"

That's when I realized that it wasn't a doll. I managed not to yelp and jump back. I had just smacked a complete stranger on her naked ass, after checking out her vulva to see if she had hair down there. I could feel my face turn from red to crimson.

The woman's head turned toward me. She was smiling broadly. "No, really! Can I have another? Make it harder this time. I want to see how the padding holds up with a good impact."

She turned her head back around, bracing for impact. I just stood there stupidly for a few seconds, torn between an urge to be polite to this stranger and to do as she asked, an urge to try to explain the situation to her, and an urge to just run.

I decided that trying to explain that I mistook her for a sex doll would just make the situation even more humiliating than it already was. My shoes weren't made for running. So I took a deep breath and spanked the woman hard on the ass.

I ended up hitting her harder than I intended. A lot of my frustration and humiliation was channeled out through my arm, and there was a loud >SMACK< sound that reverberated through the store. The place had wonderful acoustics, apparently.

Now some of the patrons in the store were turning around to look at us. Or maybe they were dolls. They were all blurring surreally together.

Having people look at me there, standing over a naked woman on a saw-horse, should have made me even more embarrassed than I already was, but I think I must have reached my maximum allowance of shame for the day. My cheeks still burned, but some part of my brain just snapped, and I decided to embrace the situation.

The woman on the saw-horse was thanking me again and asking me for another one. Even though my hand still smarted from the last hit, I swatted her again on the other cheek, making her ass bounce.

It actually felt pretty nice. I liked the feel of my palm hitting her flesh. There was a supple resilience to her body, toned muscle underneath soft skin. Also, it was nice not being on the receiving end for a change. Given the situation, I found the phrase "receiving *end*" fairly humorous, and I started to smile.

The woman apparently still wasn't done testing the merchandise, so I kept spanking her. I tried to remember the patterns and hand placements that Jaxon had used on me, to replicate them, although I avoided the more intimate areas that his hands had strayed to.

After a half-dozen more swats on her ass, the woman turned her head back around and said, "By the way, my safe word is 'lilac.'"

I made a note of that in case she ended up saying it. I felt like we were just playing around, so things shouldn't get that serious, but it was nice to know she'd let me know when she'd had enough.

The woman's butt started turning pink after a time, and a handful of people had gathered around us. I'd climbed up onto the platform by this point, to get a better angle to strike from. It was a little like being up on stage.

The people around us, men and women in varying levels of dress or nudity, were smiling appreciatively. Some of them gave occasional cheers or sounds of approval. I started to really get into things, feeding on the positive reinforcement.

A hand held out a paddle in front of me, offering it for my use. I looked down and saw a bearded man in a suit grinning up at me. He nodded. "Go on. Stacy belongs to me. We were talking about trying this one out."

Things were getting out of hand, but it was all so completely bizarre and disorienting that I just gave a mental shrug and went along with it. Besides, my hand was getting pretty sore.

I took the paddle and swished it through the air. It felt light, with little more weight than a whiffle-ball bat. I gave the woman a test swat on the ass. There was a surprisingly satisfying smack. I smacked her again, harder, and this time the paddle left her skin red where it struck.

I played around a bit. I tried to take pauses, building up anticipation the way that Jaxon had done with me. I found myself wondering what exactly he felt when he was doing this to me.

It had seemed like a big turn-on for him, but I didn't really get it. I was a little turned on, just from being in a sex shop, but spanking somebody didn't really do it for me. I tried to get a bit more inside Jaxon's head, to see what the appeal was for him.

I kind of liked the way her ass bounced when I spanked her. I liked the way that her buttocks turned into an almost wave of flesh that immediately rebounded back to its original position. I also liked the sound of it. The sound was a bit of a turn-on, actually, but I think that was mostly because it was giving me flashbacks of when Jaxon had paddled me.

He had stood behind me much like I was standing behind this woman. I'd been helpless. I'd been exposed the way she was exposed to me. My own ass had been up higher, though, and my legs more spread. I could see part of the woman's... I found myself fighting against thinking the word, but given the circumstances I decided I might as well think it: the woman's pussy.

I could see parts of the woman's pussy, but I had a feeling that mine had been more exposed to Jaxon. This woman's pussy was lower, as if she was pressing it to... Oh. She was rubbing her clit against the saw-horse as I spanked her.

I watched, both repulsed and fascinated. Clearly this was sexual for her. In my mind I'd just been playing with a stranger, but now I realized that I was helping another woman get off. Her hips moved with each swat of the paddle, and now I could recognize the movements as sexual.

I paused, uncertain if I wanted to continue with this now that I had a better idea of what exactly was going on. It would seem rude to stop, though. I kind of froze, with the paddle pulled back for another strike.

"Making new friends, I see." Jaxon's voice made me jump. I turned and saw him standing next to the bearded man. They seemed comfortable with each other. I couldn't tell if it was because they knew each other already or if it was more like when random dog owners bond over their pets playing together at the park.

"Master," I started, but I didn't have anything else to say. How could I explain this?

He nodded at the woman. "Don't keep Stacy waiting too long. Too much suspense can turn to boredom."

Oh. Okay, I guess he was fine with this. I walloped Stacy with a good one and was rewarded with a loud cry.

"Your form isn't too bad," Jaxon informed me. "But I think that coat is interfering with your swing a bit. Let me hold it for you."

I froze. There were nearly a dozen people crowded around the platform now, including Jaxon and the bearded man. I was naked underneath my coat. Jaxon wanted me to strip in front of all these people?

I couldn't make my arms or legs move.

Jaxon nodded at Stacy again, and out of reflex I paddled her again.

Jaxon leaned forward and whispered to me. "Don't embarrass me in front of my friends, slave, unless you want it to go in your punishment book."

Oh, shit.

I stood all the way upright. I looked at the crowd. Stacy wasn't the only woman here who was already exposed. There were several women who were outright nude except for their collars, and several more women who were wearing next to nothing.

A blonde in a garter belt and stockings had panties covering her privates, but she wasn't wearing a stitch above the waist. The Asian woman next to her was wearing thigh-high rubber boots and a bustier. Her breasts were covered, but her crotch was completely bare. Like Stacy, she was clean-shaven down there.

Of all the women in the store, I was actually the most over-dressed, unless I wanted to count the one in the spandex bodysuit that covered every inch of her-- including her head--but that still somehow left nothing to the imagination. Like a couple other women there, she was holding a leash with a nearly-naked man on the other end of it.

When in Rome, do as the Romans do.

I felt shaky, but I suddenly felt more out of place wearing clothing than if I was naked. Also, I didn't want another punishment to go in the book. I placed the paddle in Jaxon's waiting hand and unbuttoned my coat.

Somebody let out a loud "Woooo!" of encouragement. Stacy had turned back and was watching me expectantly. I finished unbuttoning and shrugged the coat off onto the floor.

There was some applause, and some cries of appreciation. Jaxon was beaming at me. He handed me the paddle and I went back to work on Stacy's bottom, trying to focus on the task at hand instead of the fact that I was now standing on a platform surrounded by a small crowd of strangers, wearing only a pair of high-heels.

Somehow, the fact that I was paddling a naked stranger made it better.

Pretty soon, I started to feel more comfortable. Nobody was making a big deal out of my nudity, other than a few leers and smirks. It was nothing that I hadn't put up with while wearing a nice dress to a bar, except this crowd seemed more respectful, more accepting.

It was as if they understood that I was doing this by choice, that I was going out of my way for them, and they appreciated it. They appreciated me. They didn't just take my presence or my body for granted, because I could walk off the stage at any time.

I saw Jaxon looking at me, proud of me, pleased with me, and something clicked into place. It was the same way with him. He knew that I could vanish from his life with one whisper of the safe word, and that I didn't have to be doing any of this. That was why being his "slave" didn't seem as demeaning as I would have expected. Jaxon actually respected me and appreciated my sacrifice. Real slave-masters wouldn't do that, because the slavery was involuntary.

My arm was on auto-pilot, smacking away at Stacy's increasingly blushing bottom as I was caught up in my own thoughts. I snapped out of it when I saw the bearded man approaching Stacy's head. He seemed to be watching her carefully.

Stacy's hips were moving at a steady beat, in time with the paddle. She was using the momentum from each swat to rub herself forward on the saw-horse, then rub herself back again in time for the next smack. Without realizing it, I had changed to a steadier rhythm, and the paddling had a sexual beat to it, like the thrust of a man's hips during sex.

Smack, smack, smack, smack.

I watched her torso. I could see that she was breathing faster, breathing harder. Her skin was flushed more than just where I was paddling her. Beads of sweat trickled from a few places on her body. The padded saw-horse was getting damp between her thighs.

Her breathing and body movements were growing to a crescendo. It was fascinating to watch, almost hypnotizing. It was beautiful, watching a woman near orgasm. It wasn't as much of a turn-on as watching a man, but there was a combination of aesthetic appreciation and empathy that was very satisfying.

The fact that I was the one making her move like that, the one giving her such pleasure… that was definitely getting to be a turn-on.

Another part of Jaxon's psychology seemed to click into place. This was why he did what he did--part of the reason, anyway. He liked the rush of sending such strong sensations through his slaves. He gave them pain as a way of giving them pleasure, and he got pleasure from pleasing them. At least that's the thought that occurred to me at that moment.

Stacy's crescendo was approaching its peak. Just when she seemed almost ready to climax, the bearded man clapped his hands and said, "Come!"

Stacy came as if on command. Her body stiffened, locking onto the saw-horse. Only her hips were moving, and then her head whipped back and she let out a gasp, followed by a throaty cry of pleasure that turned into a series of grunts. I felt myself grow a little wet.

I wasn't sure what to do, so I just kept paddling her, matching my pace to the rhythm of her hips as she slowed down, and then stopped. Stacy just laid there, limp, taking slow deep breaths.

"Well you're just full of surprises, aren't you?" Jaxon said. He was smiling broadly. "That was very well done. You looked so beautiful up there."

I was already grinning, but the compliment made my heart leap. He thought I was beautiful!

On impulse, I put my arms around his neck and stepped off the platform, hopping into his arms. He looked surprised, but he still caught me. He was so strong--I could feel the muscles underneath his suit, one of his arms under my shoulders and the other under my knees. I let out a little laugh of pleasure.

Then he was kissing me. His head had moved forward almost of its own accord. His eyes showed slight surprise, then they closed, and he smiled into my mouth for a brief second, and then he kissed me some more.

Like the rest of his body, his lips were strong and sure. His skillful tongue danced between my lips, exploring my mouth. I'd missed the taste of him. If our entire weekend had consisted solely of kissing, that would have been enough for me. Well, almost enough.

Okay, I'd have wanted more.

Jaxon just stood there, holding me, kissing me, for what seemed like a very long time. My senses were so completely engaged in our kiss that I didn't realize that we had an audience until I heard somebody clear their throat.

We looked up and saw Stacy and the bearded man standing there. Stacy was still completely naked except for her brown leather collar.

"Hi!" She said. She waved her fingers at me. Either she was blushing or her face was still flushed from orgasm. "I'm Stacy."

"Oh," I said, helpfully. Then my mind and my manners kicked in. "I'm Anastasia."

Jaxon set me down so that I could talk with my new playmate.

"That's a beautiful name!" Stacy seemed honestly pleased by it. I actually liked my name, but sometimes it seemed like somewhat of a cliché. Whenever I introduced myself, part of me always winced and hoped that they wouldn't bring up that trite, badly-written cartoon movie from my childhood.

"Thank you!" I said. I meant it. I realized that Stacy was probably a couple of years younger than I was. She had to be over eighteen, though, or they wouldn't have let her in the door. She really was quite pretty, right-side up and facing me.

"This is 'Stasia's first time here," Jaxon said. "I hope that Master Bernard didn't mind her borrowing you."

"Not at all!" The bearded man laughed. "Her first time here, you say? She certainly acclimatized quickly!"

Jaxon nodded his head. "Less than twenty minutes since we walked in the door. I was talking to Master R about collars when I heard the sound of a good spanking going on. I followed the sound and was surprised to see that my 'Stasia was the one dishing it out!"

'My' 'Stasia? I liked the sound of that.

I wasn't sure if I was allowed to talk to Master Bernard, but Stacy had spoken to me freely, and Jaxon hadn't objected when I had replied to her. I figured that it was safest to stick to talking to her.

"I guess you liked it?" I felt stupid asking the question. I had so many questions for her, too many to ask. I wanted to know how long she'd been a slave, what Master Bernard was like, if she was a Mayflower... Too many questions. "I'd never really spanked anybody before."

Stacy's eyes widened with surprise. She was about to speak, but Bernard cut off anything she might have said.

"Never?" He seemed shocked. "Well, you certainly do have a knack for it. If I hadn't shown up, Stacy might have come without permission, and that'd be one more for her book. She's already been a naughty girl today as it is. I swear she's trying to wear my arm out."

I wanted to ask what Stacy had done, but I didn't know if I was allowed to address Bernard, or if I had to call him 'Master' if I did, or if I was only allowed to call Jaxon that. I just ended up staring at him while I tried to think of what to do.

We were interrupted by a crashing, clattering sound. We turned toward the noise, and Stacy was standing next to a small table that had apparently been displaying a bunch of plastic bottles of lubricant. Most of the bottles were scattered on the floor.

Stacy looked Master Bernard right in the eye, smiled, and said, "Oops."

I didn't have the slightest impression that she was being genuine.

Master Bernard growled, then grabbed a riding crop from a hook on the wall. He shook his head, smiled, and said: "See what I mean?"

Then he was standing menacingly over Stacy, crop his hand, ordering her to pick up the mess that she had made. When she got on all fours to pick up the bottles, he smacked her on the back of her thigh with the crop.

"Good thing none of those spilled," he chastised her. "That would be a slippery situation!"

Jaxon gently grabbed my elbow and led me away. As we headed toward the back of the store, I noticed a woman in a French maid's outfit walk out of a side door marked "Private." She headed over to the saw-horse, produced a cloth and a spray bottle, and started cleaning it thoroughly. I wondered how many times a day she had to do that particular task.

As we moved through the aisles, the occasional customer would smile and nod at me, or give me a thumbs-up. I tried not to blush. I was getting more and more practice at that lately.

"You certainly seem to have made a good impression on our first outing." Jaxon told me. "But you shouldn't have lied to Bernard and Stacy about never spanking anybody before."

I was caught off-guard. "But... Master, that wasn't a lie. I never had spanked anybody."

Jaxon whirled me about, so that I was facing him. He looked me in the eye. "Never?"

"Never, Master."

He studied me long and hard. He seemed angry about something, but he nodded. "If not, then that's a problem in its own right."

I had no idea what he meant by that.

# CHAPTER 16

I was surprised at the selection of collars available. There were round display racks full of them, and more hanging on the walls. There was even a bin full of cheap-looking collars of various sorts.

Jaxon ignored all of these, though, and walked over to a glass display case. The collars behind the glass were all fancy and expensive-looking. Many of the collars here looked more like jewelry. Some looked like they were gold, or silver. Most of them had fancy stones or gems in them.

Jaxon pointed at one in particular. This one was made of thick leather so black that it almost looked like velvet. It looked strong, but softer than most of the other leather collars. There was a ring attached to the front of it, hanging down almost like a pendant. It looked like it was silver. On the collar itself, over the ring, was a diamond.

I could tell that it was a real diamond because of the way that it glistened, and because of the price tag. It was more than I could ever think about being able to afford, but it was beautiful.

I wanted it.

"I like it, Master." My voice was soft, respectful. I suddenly felt like I was in a high-class jewelry shop, not standing naked in the back of a sex store. "I like it a lot."

"Let's see how it looks on you, then." He spoke casually. I couldn't believe that he was serious.

"Oh, I couldn't...," I started saying. I took a step back, shaking my head. Then I remembered myself and willed my feet to stop moving. I straightened myself up. I was out of my league and out of my element. The thought of even trying on something so expensive, so beautiful, sent me into a near panic. But we were in Jaxon's world, and he was the one in charge. It was his decision, and it would be his fault if anything went horribly wrong. I sighed. "If it pleases you, Master."

The frown that had appeared at my initial reaction now disappeared. He nodded, and then motioned to the man behind the counter. The man opened the back of the glass case and took out the collar. He handed it to Jaxon.

"Turn around," Jaxon told me.

I obeyed.

He put the collar around my neck. There was a silver buckle on the back of it. Jaxon fastened it, adjusting it so that it was snug but not actually tight.

Then he led me to away from the counter, off to the side.

I walked carefully, as if the collar might shatter if I took a wrong step. I was watching my feet, and I didn't even notice where we were going until Jaxon's hand gently grabbed my jaw, guiding my head upward.

Standing in front of me were three naked women, each with the same collar. They were beautiful. They were me. Jaxon had led me to a full-length triple mirror so that I could see how I looked. Other than my jaw hanging slightly open, I looked good.

Somehow the collar made me look less naked. I was still completely exposed, but now I felt armored. I still felt like I was looking at somebody else, somebody beautiful. I felt a drop of something damp on my nose, and my vision was starting to blur. I was tearing up, starting to cry. I didn't know why.

Jaxon was standing behind me. He leaned forward, kissed my ear, and then gently nipped it. His right hand reached out, stroked my right side, and traveled up my bare chest to cup my left breast. He squeezed me gently, and he kissed my neck. I felt like I was watching it happen to somebody else. I felt a sudden tingling between my legs.

"It looks good." Jaxon used words so simple that they seemed almost profane. 'Good' just didn't cover it. He called over to the man behind the counter. "It looks good! We'll take it."

I was stunned.

"You're…," I started. "Master, you're buying this for me? I can't."

Jaxon shrugged. "I wasn't sure before, but once I saw how well the collar fit your natural beauty, I don't want you ever to take it off."

There really wasn't anything that I could say to that. I just stood there, my hand on my collar. Then I leaned in and kissed him on the cheek. No man had ever bought me a diamond before.

# CHAPTER 17

When we finally left the store, I was still wearing the collar. I was also carrying a small brown paper bag that contained a riding crop, one of those multi-tailed whips, and some items that Jaxon hadn't let me see, although he promised me that I'd get to see at least some of them later. I didn't like his smile when he said that.

We got into the back of the car and headed off. Almost as soon as the car was in motion, Jaxon was leaning over to my side of the car. I leaned toward him, expecting him to whisper something. Instead he grabbed the silver ring on the front of my collar, pulling me in for a kiss.

This time, the kiss wasn't gentle. This time he was forceful as well as passionate, as if he wanted to be sure that I belonged to him. Or as if he wanted to be sure that I knew where I belonged.

I did.

I welcomed his tongue into my mouth, then jolted in surprise as his free hand found its way between my legs. He slid his hand under my coat, up along my inner thigh. Then his fingers found me.

My gasp was muffled by his mouth, and he made a small inhalation, as if eager to absorb my very air. His fingers pet me, parted me. I was already wet.

One of his fingers slid inside of me. His palm pushed against my clit, rubbing me as his finger explored my depths. My legs spread wider of their own accord, my body hungry for more if his touch.

Soon a second finger joined the first, stretching me wider, making me feel fuller. The hand that had been holding my collar was now holding the back of my neck, pulling my mouth tightly against his. I lost myself in the sensation of kissing, of his fingers inside of me.

I stopped paying attention to my surroundings. I lost track of time. It was like I was hypnotized by what he was doing to me, by the pleasure that he was inflicting on me. Eventually I noticed that the car was stopped, that we were parked outside a restaurant.

Jaxon pulled away from me then. I let out a frustrated moan of disappointment as his fingers abandoned their home inside of my body. My hips still moved slightly, instinctively, even after there was nothing to rub up against.

Jaxon opened the brown paper sack that contained the merchandise we had purchased at the sex store. I heard the tearing of plastic, and his hands busied themselves doing something inside the bag.

I wanted to ask him what he was doing, but I didn't have permission to speak. I also had an idea what he was up to. He was preparing one of the mystery toys that he had purchased. I fought my own frustration and impatience, and managed to sit there quietly until he was done.

Eventually he produced what looked like a small rubber egg. He grinned at me, and then the hand with the egg moved back between my legs. I could feel him rubbing it against my slick entrance. Then I could feel him sliding it inside of me.

I'd never had any kind of toy inside of me before. The sensation was odd, but pleasing. It wasn't as nice as Jaxon's fingers had been, but there was a sensual squirminess from having it there. Jaxon grinned at me some more and then pulled away, returning to his side of the car.

"Shall we?" he asked. Without waiting for an answer, he opened his door and he stepped out.

What? Were we going inside? I still had the toy in me.

I got out of the car. I took a couple of cautious steps. The toy didn't seem ready to fall out or anything, although I could kind of feel it move a bit inside of me when I moved.

Jaxon was looking at me impatiently. I walked around the car to join him. He put out his arm, and I took it. Did he really expect me to eat dinner wearing only a coat and high heels?

Jaxon stopped walking, and I mentally breathed a sigh of relief. We were going to turn back around, get back in the car, and leave.

We didn't, though. Instead, Jaxon reached behind my neck and unfastened my collar. I had forgotten that it was even there. He put it into his pocket, then held out my arm. We resumed walking.

I saw the name of the restaurant, and I wanted to turn and run. We were at 'The Centerpiece', a rather high-end dining establishment that I'd been wanting to go to for some time, but I couldn't ever afford. Jaxon pulled me along with him through the front doors, where we were greeted by a maitre d'.

He seemed to know Jaxon. He offered to take my coat, but Jaxon just shook his head and the man backed away. My blood was rushing so loudly in my ears that I couldn't hear what was said, but the man led us to a booth in the back of the restaurant.

The lights were dimmer here, the lighting more intimate and more likely to conceal the fact that I was naked underneath my coat. Jaxon acted perfectly casual about the whole thing. I was mortified, expecting at any moment for somebody to point out that I was under-dressed.

Nobody did. The waiter came to the table, and Jaxon ordered us some drinks and some appetizers. He knew what kind of wine I liked: sweet and red. He ordered something appropriate for me, then ordered something dry and white for himself.

For appetizers, he ordered escargot. I fought not to frown. Escargot was snails. I hoped that he wasn't expecting me to eat any.

For a main course, Jaxon ordered the surf 'n turf for both of us: steak and lobster. On one hand I was mildly insulted that he didn't let me pick my own food. On the other hand, I adored both steak and lobster, and couldn't often afford either.

The waiter left, and we sat awkwardly for a couple of minutes. Well, I sat awkwardly, because I was unable to speak without permission. Jaxon seemed perfectly content and comfortable in the silence. Normally, on a real date, this was the point where we'd make small-talk. Without that option, I felt uncomfortable and vulnerable.

I kept waiting for him to say something, but he didn't. He just sat there, looking at me with those deep blue eyes. I tried looking back, but eventually I was the one to turn away. It seemed like the man was incapable of blinking. He could be so unnerving.

I looked down at the table for a while, then felt foolish doing that. I looked back up at him, and he was still looking at me. Not exactly staring, just looking. I wondered what his game was.

I looked away again, trying to see if the waiter was coming with our food. He wasn't. I looked back at Jaxon, who was still looking at me. I kept wanting to talk, to break the silence, but I still didn't have permission to speak. Even though I was physically free, I somehow felt just as trapped as when I had been cuffed to Jaxon's table, just as helpless.

Minutes passed.

I started to feel my mind curl in on itself, to feel myself surrender in some strange way. Like with the clothespins, there was no way to escape the discomfort of the situation. Nothing that I could do short of getting up and leaving entirely would relieve my suffering.

I felt myself once again enter that strange state of submission, a state where I was willing to do anything just to be freed from the discomfort, but where the discomfort itself somehow started to become almost comfortable. How could he have this effect on me without actually doing anything?

I gave myself up to that strange state, letting myself ease into a state of quasi-comfortable readiness where I was both relaxed and alert without really being either of those two things. Eventually, I reached a balanced ambivalence where I was able to simply sit, looking back at Jaxon patiently.

I didn't look him in the eyes, but I looked at him near his eyes, almost meeting his gaze but not quite.

This carefully balanced state lasted about six heartbeats before it was interrupted.

"Tell me, slave." His voice startled me. Just when I had gotten used to the silence, he changed the game. "Have you ever been to this establishment before?"

It took a moment before I remembered where I had left my own voice. "No, Master."

"That's a shame," he said. "It really is quite nice."

I wasn't sure if he was prompting me to continue talking or not. I dared to risk it, rather than to fall back into that dreadful silence we had just escaped from. I wondered if he used this sort of game professionally, to unnerve opponents during negotiations and such.

"I wanted to come here," I said. "But I never really could afford it."

Shit! Did I call him 'master' in there? I think I forgot. It didn't seem natural that time. Did that matter?

There were so many subtleties and grey areas when it came to his rules.

Jaxon took no notice of my slip, if it was one. He nodded, then looked as if he was about to speak. But whatever he might have said was cut off by the arrival of the waiter.

The waiter proudly presented an ornate metal tray that had twelve round indentations in it, as if it was meant for carrying golf balls. Instead of golf balls, though, each of the twelve places held a large colorful shell that held some kind of buttery sauce and a brownish-black object inside.

Oh, goody. Our snails were finally here. They almost looked like little cooked mushrooms.

The smell of garlic and melted butter hit me, and I realized how hungry I was. The dish looked surprisingly appetizing, but I was wary. I just didn't like the idea of it.

"Wonderful," Jaxon said. He seemed to be completely serious. The waiter smiled and left us alone with our snails.

Jaxon looked at me, studying my face. I looked at the snails. They came with tiny little forks, apparently designed specifically for pulling the little molluscs out of their shells. Unusual tastes required unusual tools, I supposed.

"You don't have to try them," Jaxon told me. "You're an adult and you're here of your own free will. If the dish seems to strange to you, too daunting, then you don't have to partake."

I felt a sigh of relief. I also felt my mouth water a bit. The smell of the garlic and butter was enticing.

"But," Jaxon continued, "I think that if you can find the fortitude to try something new, to break out of your own little shell as it were, that you may find it unexpectedly rewarding. I won't order you, but it would please me if you would give it a taste."

Crap. I realized that I wanted to please him, that I was willing to eat a snail if it would make him happy. It was turning out to be quite the weekend of new experiences.

Still, I hesitated. I just hated the idea of eating snails. It just seemed… gross.

Jaxon watched me in my indecision, and he spoke. "It's all just appearances, Stasia. You're bound up in your own perceptions, a slave to the things that you have been taught are normal. You can't look at the escargot without seeing snails, and you've been taught that snails are gross little creatures, and that it's not normal to eat them. But snails have been eaten by humans since prehistoric times and were considered to be a delicacy since the Romans. The right snails, cooked the right way, at least."

I could see what he was saying, but I couldn't get past the fact that he was wanting me to eat a snail.

"It's all just perception, though," he continued. "I saw your eyes when I ordered our main course, and I could tell that you approved. Whether or not you choose to try the escargot, in a matter of minutes you'll be enthusiastically chowing down on a giant sea-bug and the seared muscle tissue of a cow."

He let me digest that thought for a while.

"There are people who would find that disgusting. Disgust, like beauty, exists purely in the eye of the beholder." He was looking at me with those blue eyes again, gazing nto me. I saw something there, some hint of strange desperation as if the subject we were discussing was of deep importance to him. Did I imagine that? "Let go of your preconceptions, Stasia. Let go of whatever other associations you have and look at things again. Do you smell the butter? The garlic? The thyme and other spices? There's an entire world of flavor there, and all that is keeping you from savoring it is your own prejudice."

He took one of the tiny forks off of the tray. He skewered one of the little mushroom-looking snails. He held it out to me. "I ask you to give it a try. Not just for me, but for you. An honest try. Don't just swallow this like you would a bitter pill, don't tighten up in anticipation and just endure it. Embrace it. Savor it.

Open yourself up and experience it for what it is, not for what you're afraid it might be."

If Jaxon ever tired of law, he could make an absolute killing working for the escargot industry. I had no idea that he loved eating snails so much.

There was a twinkle in his eyes that I tried to match in my own as I leaned forward and opened my mouth to his offering with gratitude. I tried to open myself completely, to engage all of my senses in readiness for whatever sensations were about to hit me. I lowered my defenses and took my first taste of escargot.

I tasted butter, garlic, and herbs. The snail itself was mostly chewy, essentially flavorless. I let out a loud gasp of shock and pleasure, not from the pleasant flavor of the food in my mouth, but from something else entirely.

A few patrons at other tables turned their heads to look at me, to see what why I made such a noise, but it wasn't anything that they could see. They turned back to their tables, oblivious of what was happening to me. I gripped my own table with both hands, holding on tightly.

I had forgotten that I still had the little egg-shaped toy inside of me. I was caught completely off-guard when it started to vibrate and buzz, sending rippling waves of erotic pleasure through my lower regions.

The toy was a vibrator, and Jaxon had a remote. He was smirking like a stage magician who was pleased with his own trick. I glared at him, took a deep breath, and let go of the table. The little egg kept pulsing away inside of me, stirring sensations that I didn't feel were entirely appropriate for public dining.

"You…" I couldn't formulate a sentence that described how I felt. No, wait… I could. "You jerk!"

"That's 'you jerk, *Master*.'" Jaxon smiled. "I won't mark this one down in your punishment book, though. I'll exercise my right to punish you right here and now."

His hand did something under the table and the vibration inside of me increased. I had never used any kind of vibrator before. It was an almost overpowering sensation, even though the speed didn't seem to be very fast.

I silently glared at Jaxon as I fought to compose myself. Jaxon smiled back pleasantly, as if nothing was wrong. Both of his hands were back above the table.

"It can be fun, can't it?" he asked. "Trying new things?"

The taste of escargot lingered in my empty mouth. I must have swallowed the food out of reflex. Suddenly, I felt stubborn.

I picked up the little fork, stabbed a garlic-buttered snail, then put the snail in my mouth. It really was quite tasty, even if most of the taste was in the sauce.

"I knew you'd want more, once you tried it," Jaxon said. His hand went under the table again, and the pulsing increased again.

It felt incredible, but I didn't want this feeling in a public place. It wasn't appropriate. I felt like we were in some sort of contest, though, and I hated losing contests.

I speared and ate another snail. The vibration sped up even further.

By the time I had eaten the sixth snail, I was completely over any revulsion I'd originally had at the thought. They were food like any other kind of food. Granted, I was pretty distracted by then.

The vibrating egg was making my body throb with pleasure. I had to fight to sit still; I wanted to squirm in my seat. I told myself that I was trying to adjust to make the sensation lessen, and that was true, but it wasn't the whole truth. I also wanted to make it stronger.

Jaxon watched me happily as he picked up the other tiny fork and started in on his half of the escargot. He enjoyed watching the little telltale twitches and spasms as I worked to fight off the pleasure, while also not wanting to escape it entirely.

I was caught in a terrible, wonderful position between too much pleasure and not enough of it. The pleasure kept building up, threatening to make me succumb, to make me just give in and let the impending orgasm take me. I would cry out and I would thrash, and everybody would stare at me. My hands clenched the table in preparation for both humiliation and ecstasy. I would try to remain calm when it happened, but there would be no way for me to fool everybody who heard me, who saw me when the time came. Some of them would know.

Just when I thought that I couldn't fight it any longer, the waiter came back to the table carrying a tray with two salad bowls. He asked if I wanted fresh ground pepper, and I knew that if I opened my mouth to speak, I'd lose control and end up moaning instead.

Then the internal pulsations slowed a few degrees, and suddenly I was in control again. I could speak, so I did: "Yes, please."

The entire time we ate our salads, I kept expecting Jaxon to increase the speed again. Any time he moved his hand even close to the edge of the table, I'd flinch, expecting his hand to disappear below the table to that remote control he must have, returning the toy to the tortuous tempo that it had been at before.

Jaxon took advantage of that, keeping his hand near the edge of the table most of the time while we ate our salad. We didn't talk, just ate in silence, but I realized that I was enjoying myself. The tantalizing throb of the toy was somewhat nerve-wracking given the environment, but now that I was more used to it, it was quite pleasant.

Shortly, the main course arrived. The food was excellent, and Jaxon allowed me to enjoy my meal in relative peace. Although he did move his hand under the table a few times, just to mess with me, he didn't increase the vibrations to their previous level.

On the car ride home, after dinner, Jaxon kissed me again. His hands explored my body, delving into my coat and caressing the bare flesh underneath. He had set the toy to its lowest setting, I think, and by the time we got back to Jaxon's penthouse, I had been so thoroughly teased that I was ready to explode.

Once we were inside, with the green doors locked behind us, Jaxon ordered me to remove my coat. I did, gladly. Once the coat was off, Jaxon put my collar back on me, the soft leather clinging to my skin like a lover's kiss.

I started toward the bedroom, but Jaxon tsked and shook his head. He produced a black leather leash from somewhere and attached it to my collar. Then he started walking away from the bedroom.

I had to either follow or dig in my heels and fight the leash. I followed. At least he wasn't trying to make me crawl this time.

Jaxon turned down a short hall that had a heavy wooden door at the end. He pulled a key out of his pocket, unlocked the door, and led me inside a room that I hadn't seen before.

The first thing that I noticed was a padded sawhorse like the one that I'd seen in the store earlier. The second thing that I noticed was that the room was completely furnished with similar devices. Jaxon had brought me to his own personal dungeon.

# CHAPTER 18

The next thing I knew, Jaxon was leading me to a pair of sturdy wooden posts in the middle of the room. Leather cuffs hung from a pair of short chains, one on each post. He led me between the two posts, then cuffed each of my wrists so that I was secure.

He unclipped the leash and walked a short distance away. I wondered what he was up to, but I didn't ask. Was he going to paddle me again?

Jaxon returned with a thin, leather-bound book. I couldn't see the pages, but he told me what was on them.

"This," he said, "is your punishment book. As I said before, your every misdeed or disobedience will go in that book unless, as I did at dinner earlier, I exercise my right to punish you on the spot."

Oh, yeah. The punishment book. I felt my libido cool a bit. I wasn't in for sex, not yet anyway. I was in for a paddling, or maybe something worse.

"Every evening you will be punished," Jaxon continued. "Tonight you will be punished for five things. You neglected to address me by my title on three different occasions. Four, including dinner, but that transgression has been dealt with."

He paused, then continued. "For each of these transgressions, I will institute a handicap during your evening punishment session. For the first failure to address me properly, I will blindfold you. For the second transgression, you will receive an anal plug. For the third transgression, you will be gagged."

Anal plug? That didn't sound good. I instinctively pulled at my chains, but there was no way I could escape. Not unless I used the safe word anyway. Wait... how was I supposed to use the safe word if I had a gag in my mouth? I tried to get Jaxon's attention with my eyes.

Jaxon looked at me impatiently, annoyed. He continued, answering the unasked question.

"For this session, your safe word will be to stamp your right foot three times on the ground. If you do that, then I will remove your gag and determine what the issue is. For this session, because it will be particularly intense, and because there will be a gag, you may use this safe word without ending our weekend entirely. If you stamp your foot three times, that may end the session, but it will not necessarily end our time together."

Crap. This was going to be rough. I was determined not to use the safe word unless I had to, but it was nice to know that I wasn't going to be risking everything if I broke down tonight. What exactly did he have planned?

"On two occasions today," Jaxon intoned, "you had orgasms without my permission. This is a serious offense. I cannot properly train you to come on command if you continue to steal your release without permission."

I wasn't entirely sure what he was talking about with the "come on command" bit, but it was nice to know that there was some kind of reason for that rule, at least.

"For your first stolen orgasm, I will issue twelve strokes to your breasts with a flogger. For the second stolen orgasm, I will issue twelve strokes to your ass with a flogger."

While we were in the store, I had eventually learned that those multi-tailed whips were called "floggers." Well, some of them were "cats." I didn't really know the difference. I pictured Jaxon whipping me with one of those things and I tensed up.

Jaxon walked behind me. I couldn't see what he was doing. He rummaged around behind me for what felt like several minutes, leaving me with nothing to do but to contemplate my impending punishment. The more I thought about it, the worse it seemed that it was going to be.

Jaxon eventually returned to view. He was holding a number of objects in one hand, and a small wooden case in the other. He set all of the items on a nearby table and spread them out where I could see them.

There was a leather flogger with an ornate black and red handle. There was a blindfold that reminded me of a sleeping mask that my mother used to wear at night, only this one was black instead of green. There was the brown wooden case. Then there was an odd contraption that looked like a horse's bit.

Jaxon opened up the wooden case. Inside were a variety of objects that looked like oddly shaped dildos. They looked too narrow at the tip, and too wide at the bottom, and there was a skinny neck at the base followed by a much wider flared-out part.

After some thought, I realized that those must be anal plugs. There was a series of sizes, ranging from one about the size of my finger to one about the size of my forearm. I said a mental prayer that he was going to use one from the smaller end of the spectrum.

Jaxon picked up the thing that looked like a bit and approached me. The bar was wrapped in leather. The leather had old teeth marks in it. I realized that this was the gag he had mentioned.

Jaxon held the bar up to my mouth, his other hand on my jaw, guiding my mouth open. I thought about refusing, then decided that obedience was simplest. I could always stomp my foot and get out of all of this.

Once the leather-bound bar was firmly in my teeth, Jaxon strapped the device in place with the belt, securing it behind my head. I didn't like it, but it wasn't too bad.

Next, Jaxon returned to the table to pick up the blindfold. He placed that over my eyes, and I could no longer see what he was doing.

I could hear his footsteps return to the table. I heard the movement of objects on the table. Then I heard his voice.

"You said your threshold level was seven, correct? Well, then you ought to be able to handle this one without any problem. Right?" He sounded almost as if he was taunting me. Had he seen through my lies at some point? If he was angry with me, I was in a very, very bad position.

"Let's help get you ready," Jaxon said. Then the toy inside of me sped up, vibrating furiously, sending shivers of reluctant pleasure speeding through me. My legs nearly buckled with surprise and sensation. It was actually a good thing that my arms were chained--I used them to help stay upright.

I could feel Jaxon's presence in front of me. I'm not sure how. It might have been his body heat, or it might have been some miniscule level of light peeking around the edges of my mask, allowing his shadow to betray his presence.

Then I felt his warm breath on my breast, just a slight exhalation, just enough to make me shudder. Then he did the same thing to the other breast. My nipples started to harden, seeking out more of Jaxon's warmth.

Jaxon toyed with me for a while. He would pull back, and I would feel nothing. Then he would find some way to stimulate me, to tease me cruelly with the promise of sex and satisfaction.

His fingers would pluck at my nipples. His tongue would caress my flesh. His hand would cup one of my curves. His lips would kiss my skin.

With the blindfold on, there was no way to see him coming. With my arms chained, there was no way to fend him off. It was like being at the mercy of a seductive ghost. My senses strained to find him, to anticipate him, but he was beyond their reach.

A lick. A kiss. A flick. Then his mouth was on my nipple, sucking on it eagerly, his tongue finding all the right places. Pleasure blossomed in my breast and I let out a gasp. Then he was gone again.

I expected him to move to the other breast, and my nipple grew harder as it hungrily waited for him. Instead, I felt his hands on my hips, and he pressed his face between my legs.

His tongue immediately found my clitoris, stroking it up and down. My knees weakened again. I spread my legs further so he could have better access. I was having trouble balancing in the high heels that I still had on, the only clothing I wore, unless I counted the collar, the gag, and the blindfold.

His fingers found my secret flesh and penetrated me with ease. I was already so wet. I had been wet since before we even got to the restaurant. I made a soft sound of joy to have part of him inside of me again.

He had two fingers inside of me, I think. I couldn't be certain. His tongue kept licking me. The toy buzzed around next to his fingers. I was getting close to the edge already.

He pulled his fingers out but continued to lick me. Without the penetration, though, it wasn't enough to let me finish. Which was good, considering the fact that I was already being punished for coming without permission.

Then Jaxon's fingers slid behind me, slipped into the crevice there. They found my other opening, and they prodded at its entrance. His fingers were still slick from being inside of me, and the lubricant helped one of them slip into me again, via a different door.

I moaned into my bit.

I still wasn't used to being penetrated that way. My only experience was from the night before, when Jaxon used his thumb. The finger was different, longer.

It penetrated deeper. I could feel Jaxon exploring there, moving his finger cautiously around.

The finger and the toy were only separated by thin veils of flesh, and the presence of the finger pushed a bit on the toy, making the vibrations more intense. I sank my teeth into the bit, emitting muffled sounds.

Jaxon's fingers abandoned me, left me wanting more. I got more. As soon as his fingers left, an object replaced them. It slid into me with slow deliberation, centimeter by centimeter.

I remembered the larger of the anal plugs that Jaxon had showed me, and I remembered him taunting me. I tried to pull away, to keep it from entering me, afraid that he picked one that was far too big for me. I was afraid that I might rip.

As it slid into me, though, I realized that it had to be one of the smaller ones. It wasn't much bigger than Jaxon's finger had been. The base grew wider and wider until I was stretched out almost painfully, then it suddenly narrowed, leaving my sphincter frantically clutching that narrow part before the flare.

I was pinned by it. My body couldn't accept it further inside, and my body couldn't reject it. My sphincter was held there, open, muscles clenching the invader desperately. The sensation was strange, but arousing.

Now the toy was buzzing against the plug, through those thin walls of tissue. Both objects felt enormous. The buzzing decreased a bit, right before I came, just enough to keep me from coming. Jaxon and his damned remote.

His tongue had pulled away from me at some point, probably when I was distracted by the plug entering me. His hands stroked my thighs, then my buttocks. Then he pulled away and I was left there, completely helpless.

Then I heard the whip. I could hear the many tendrils of the flogger whooshing through the air. Jaxon was taking practice swings, letting me hear what was coming for me. The noises stopped, and suddenly those tendrils were draped across my flesh. They moved over my breasts, lightly tantalizing them with their caress.

The feel of the leather strips dancing over my skin made my nipples tingle, and the tingling seemed to spike down through my chest, merging with the tinglings that the plug and the toy were giving me. These little streaks of pleasure pulsed together, sending sweet sensations swelling through my body.

The leather strips left my breasts, leaving me just enough time to be disappointed before the leather came back with a vengeance.

Whap.

It was a fairly light hit to the side of my left breast, the flogger's strips feeling almost like a single slap from an open hand. The blow was light enough to mostly just register as more sensation, and in the highly aroused state I was in, more sensation was good sensation.

Whap.

My right breast this time, slightly harder. I could tell the difference between the body of the straps and the tips. The tips dug in more, stung more, as if they had more force than the rest. I exhaled through my mouth, past the leather bit.

Whap.

The underside of my right breast this time, the flogger's tips stinging my flesh, even past the pleasure that my body was feeling. My breast bounced a bit from the impact, and there was something about the movement that felt pleasurable in spite of the sting.

Whap.

I had been expecting him to hit the underside of my left breast, to keep to the pattern, but this time the tips lashed out at my right nipple, flicking it painfully. I cried out, biting down on the gag. My nipples were still sore, still sensitive from the clothespins earlier in the day.

Whap.

My other nipple this time. I chomped down on my bit, trying not to cry out, but noise still escaped me. After the sting came sharp pain, but also a small amount of pleasure. My breasts were ready for sex, aching for it, and they accepted this attention as an acceptable substitute.

Whap!

The inside of my left breast, again with just the tips. This one was hard, and it felt like a dozen bees stinging me all at once. I let some of the pain escape through my mouth, along with a muffled scream, just in time for...

Whap!

A blow landed on the underside of my left breast, my flesh bounding upward, then rebounding back into place.

Whap! Whap!

The outsides of my breasts again. What a contrast there was between the gentleness of the initial strikes--barely taps--and the painful assault that this had become.

Nothing.

Silence.

My breasts felt warm, burning from my blood flowing into the assaulted area. My nipples were hard and I could feel streaks of pain decorating my chest. My senses were straining, anticipating, trying to prepare for the next...

WHAP!

The flogger's tips struck the inside curve of my right breast, stinging like needles. I screamed out in surprise, my mouth opened wide against the bit that barricaded it.

WHAP! WHAP!

Full-bodied strokes, so close together that they might almost have been one. These struck my entire breasts, the leather lashes licking around the outer curves, the tips of the tendrils sending scorching fire into me.

I braced myself for the next blows, but no more came.

Instead, Jaxon's voice boomed out of the darkness. "That is your first twelve strikes. The next twelve will begin shortly. Use your respite to meditate on your wrongdoings."

Meditate? I couldn't even think, couldn't feel anything other than the burning pain in my breasts. All of my awareness was focused on that, on the pain in my stiffened nipples, the heat in my tortured skin.

It was like Jaxon had added an exclamation point to that part of my body, like my breasts had been underlined. My senses screamed at me, telling me how urgent it was to feel absolutely everything that was going on there, to experience and analyze every drop of pleasure and pain.

Then other sensations began to intrude. The toy, buzzing away. The plug, stretching me, filling me. My wrists, sore from where I'd fought the cuffs to escape. All these sensations and more began filling me up, overwhelming me.

I felt like I was going to cry. I felt like I was going to come. I didn't know which would be the bigger relief.

"Wrongdoings." Jaxon's voice echoed in my head, my awareness focusing on just that one word. He didn't even know. He still seemed unaware that I had lied my way into his home, into his bed. He didn't understand how wrong my doings had been.

I accepted the pain, just let it wash through me, hoping that it would cleanse me of some of the guilt that I felt at using him, at abusing his trust. He'd known me for two years, and he'd liked me, and he'd trusted me, and I had abused that trust out of my own selfish need to be with him.

I'd misrepresented myself, pretended that I was something that I was not. I had known going in that

Jaxon's love was not for normal girls, not for me, but I had disguised myself, a sheep in wolf's clothing, and when that disguise wore off, how could Jaxon help but look at what I'd done with anything other than disgust and outrage?

Jaxon was playing games, little nasty sex games. He was punishing me for minor transgressions in a system set up where punishment was all but unavoidable, because punishment was what everybody wanted. The sadists wanted to hurt, and the masochists wanted to be hurt.

I only wanted Jaxon, but the insane way that I'd gone about trying to get him actually warranted this kind of punishment. More words floated through my brain, not Jaxon's words this time, but somebody else's, somebody from long, long ago.

"The Prince of Wands," the fortune-teller had told me. "A man of discipline… a co-worker…In order for the relationship to work out, you'll have to be brave, and you'll have to make sure that the two of you have clear communication between you."

I had been brave. I had been brave to the point of utter foolishness. What I hadn't done was to communicate clearly. I had lied, and all the pain that I suffered at Jaxon's hands was a result of that lie. I focused on the pain in my breasts, opened myself to it, and felt it wash away some of my guilt.

I hadn't thought about the fortune-teller's prediction in a long time, but it all came back to me now, and I felt with all my heart that Jaxon was my prince, that he was the one that I was supposed to be with. I feared with all my heart that I had messed it all up by starting things off with lies.

My heart latched onto what Jaxon had said earlier, that he might like me for the week. That was the next step. If I could get him to accept me for the week, then we might have a chance. He might learn to love me before our time was up, and that just might mean that our time wouldn't have to be up. One week might lead to another, and another, leading to months then years.

Did I even want that, after all he'd done to me? Yes. Very much so. Maybe now more than ever.

I had miniature flashbacks of Jaxon feeding me fruit, of Jaxon falling asleep in bed with me, of Jaxon's smile as he teased me during dinner. A shudder of pleasure went through my body, the toy continuing its relentless play inside of me.

Understanding broke through me, as sharp and clear as broken glass. I had to come clean, had to confess my true wrongdoings to Jaxon. I had to let him know everything before the weekend was up. He was going to find out anyway, and even if he wasn't, I didn't want our foundation to be based on lies.

I knew what he was. I knew what he was into, and I could accept him. He needed to know what I'd done, and he needed to know that I was a normal girl. If I could accept him, then surely he could accept me.

The leather tendrils of the flogger caressed the curve of my ass. Jaxon was letting them dangle down from the handle, draping them across my flesh. It was time for my punishment to continue.

Jaxon teased me like that for a time. He used the whip to pet me, to tickle and tantalize until my body was eager for more. He used his hands as well, slapping and pinching my bottom until I was on red alert, that sweet state of awful anticipation where pleasure and pain blurred. Then he struck.

Whap. Whap.

A blow on one buttock, then a pause. Then another blow on the other buttock. Not hard blows, but harder than he'd used on my breasts starting out.

Whap.

A gentle blow, striking down along the crevice between my cheeks. The blow itself was almost gentle, but the tips of the tendrils lashed down between my parted legs, striking the tender flesh between my thighs. A jolt of painful ecstasy made me cry out past my gag.

Whap.

Another blow, same as the last one. I squirmed. I moved my hips, trying to avoid another blow like that, eager for another one to land.

Whap! Whap!

A blow to the each buttock, the body of the tendrils striking my bottom, the tips of the whips licking around my curves to sting the sides of my ass. I was almost dancing now, moving mindlessly in my pain. I was biting down on the bit, letting my surplus of sensation sneak out of my body in groans and moans.

Nothing. A pause that threw my body off-balance, made my senses stumble and reel.

Whap. Whap! Whap. Whap!

A series of blows, each striking new flesh on my ass, keeping by body confused. The pain of the whip was blurring with the pleasure of the toy and the plug. My mind was receding, consciousness fading until feeling replaced thought and all that I could do was experience.

Whap!!

I screamed when this one landed, not just from the sheer force of the blow, but because Jaxon must have dialed the toy up to eleven. The buzz inside of me turned into tremors, then an earthquake that sent shockwaves of pleasure rippling through me.

I was going to come. It was all too much. I could feel my body trying to throw itself off the brink, into that blissful abyss. I hadn't gotten permission to come, though, so I fought it. I focused on the pain, trying to shut out the pleasure, but my body could no longer tell which was which.

Whap!!!

A final blow, across the fullness of my flesh. It felt like the whip had hit my entire ass. At the same time the blow landed, Jaxon shouted out, "Come!"

And I did.

I exploded into a shrieking, thrashing mess, my legs buckling out from under me as waves of pleasure crashed through me. That last blow, and Jaxon's command to come, were enough to hurl me over the brink, and it felt like I was falling down an endless pit of pleasure and pain.

Then I came again.

Jaxon had stopped hitting me, but the mechanical marvel inside of me was merciless. I felt like I was shaking apart, like the earthquakes of pleasure were going to drive me to pieces. I was whipped, pinned, chained, gagged, and exhausted.

My wrists started to hurt from supporting my weight. Jaxon was behind me, lifting me up, an arm under my chest, and another on my hips. I wanted to thank him, but instead I gasped as an aftershock went through me.

Jaxon's hand moved to cup my breast. His other hand moved between my legs. His body was pressed up against me from behind. His fingers found my clit and pinched my nipple at the same time that his mouth gently bit my neck.

I didn't come again, but my second orgasm blossomed into new life, making my body buck and heave in ecstasy for what felt like minutes. Jaxon's teeth had released my neck, and as he held me helplessly in the throes of bliss, he kept whispering into my ear, "Good slave. Good slave. Good slave."

Eventually the waves stopped crashing through me, my body stopped quaking, and Jaxon's fingers stopped working on me. He used the remote, and the toy stopped buzzing inside of me.

As I dangled in my chains, too tired to move, Jaxon pet me, soothed me. He knelt down and his fingers slid inside of me to retrieve the toy. Next, he slowly withdrew the plug from my ass, leaving me feeling empty on two counts.

Jaxon undid the cuffs holding my wrists. He helped me walk a short distance, then lay me face-down on a padded table. I let out a weak moan. Jaxon left, then returned. I felt him rubbing lotion onto the wounded flesh of my behind.

I realized that I was crying, not just from the pain but from the release. There was something emotional going on inside of me. Some kind of ancient scabs had been picked. I felt emotionally raw, but clean and ready to heal.

Jaxon cared for me, comforted me. He massaged me from my forehead to my toes, uttering soothing sounds and encouragements. At some point I must have simply gone to sleep from exhaustion, because the next thing I knew, I was back in the bed, alone, and it was morning.

# CHAPTER 19

I lay there for a time, with the memories of all the things that happened the previous day popping in and out of my mind until my brain could make sense of most of them.

I'd had sex with Jaxon. Lots of sex. I'd pleasured him with my mouth in the shower. He'd taken me in the bedroom. We'd had sex standing up, then continued on the bed, then rested, then had sex again.

Oh, my god. I remembered spanking that girl in the store, making her come with a paddle. I blushed. Two days ago, I wouldn't have believed that any of this would ever be anything that I could be involved in. I hadn't had sex with another woman, but I had made a woman come while Jaxon watched.

That was so strange. I didn't know what to do with it. I shoved it away, into the back of my mind, and I focused on Jaxon.

I couldn't help but smile as I thought about the insane sex I had with Jaxon. I remembered the way that his strong arms lifted me up and down on him, like the weight of my body was nothing. I remembered coming as he whipped me, and then him caring for me afterward.

I wanted to sit up but, as I tried, the soreness of my body let me know how much of a toll the flogging had taken. My muscles were sore and my flesh was on fire in places. The smile turned into a wince, and I tried to take stock of my wounds.

One of the pains in the ass about… well, about getting pains in my ass, was that I couldn't see the damage very well. There were red marks on my breasts and on the parts of my butt that I could see. I wasn't sure how the bruises from my first night were healing up.

My entire body felt sore, like I'd been hit by a freight train then lay on the tracks as a few dozen cars rolled over me. I felt like I needed a day or two just to heal. Maybe the week-long contract wasn't a good thing.

That's when I remembered that I'd come to the decision to tell Jaxon, to let him know that I was a phony. I had to tell him before the week started. The guilt was tearing me up, and the suspense of having this secret hanging over my head wasn't doing me any good either.

That's when Jaxon, speak of the devil, entered the room. He must have heard me stirring.

"Good morning, sunshine. Sleep well?" He bent over me and kissed my head.

"Yes, Master. Thank you, I did." Should I tell him now? Could I? It didn't seem like the right time, somehow.

"I've prepared breakfast. We'll be eating on the couch while we watch a movie."

A movie? That was fine with me. I was too sore to do much more than sit right now, and watching a movie seemed refreshingly normal. Or so I thought.

Jaxon led me to another side room off of the main area. This one seemed to be designed specifically for watching movies. There was a massive screen that took up most of one wall, and a number of comfortable looking couches and chairs all facing it.

This struck me as a bit odd, because it looked like the room was designed for a crowd of people, but I somehow had trouble picturing Jaxon just hanging out here with a bunch of friends. I wondered if he had many real friends.

Jaxon sat on a plush oversized couch, and he patted the seat next to him as if he was letting a pet know that it was okay to get on the furniture this time. I realized that he meant that for me, so I sat down next to him. The cushion was soft, and I ended up leaning onto him.

He put his arm around me and pulled me close. For just a moment, it was like we were boyfriend and girlfriend, just hanging out, watching a movie.

There was a tray of food on the coffee table in front of us. I reached out to grab a grape, and Jaxon slapped my hand. He glared at me, then explained, "I'm going to be feeding you this morning. Any sustenance you get will be from me."

Oh. Okay, we were doing that again. At least I wasn't cuffed this time.

Jaxon leaned forward and grabbed a bunch of grapes. He started feeding them to me, one by one. It was still weird, but nice.

After the grapes came little pieces of cheese. After the cheese came some type of puff pastry with cooked egg in the middle. There was orange juice to drink, and I had the impression that Jaxon had squeezed it himself. He'd bring the glass up to my mouth after every few bites and tilt the glass so that I could drink.

He fed me by hand until I was full, then started the movie.

The feeding thing was so weird. I got that it was a control thing, but it seemed so backwards, like he was exercising control by serving me instead of by making me serve him. Wasn't the slave supposed to feed the master grapes, not the other way around?

I wasn't complaining.

When the movie started, there was a sound like the cackle of a witch, and then spooky music started playing. It looked like he was having me watch some sort of horror movie, apparently about witches or something.

The movie opened up with six beautiful, scantily-clad women all making out with each other, and I realized that this wasn't going to be a horror movie after all. We were watching porn. Somehow, I should have known.

I'd never really watched a pornographic movie before, and I was morbidly curious. Good thing, because pretty soon I was watching an all-girl orgy unfold on the screen. I felt Jaxon watching me watch the movie, and I felt like I was being tested.

As I watched the women writhe and contort together on the screen, I felt a warmth stirring down below, felt myself start to get physically aroused. I only started to get aroused, though--I didn't quite get there all the way.

It was like part of my mind recognized that sex was going on and tried to identify with the girls on the screen, but another part of my mind just kept asking, "Where's the man?"

I apparently needed both halves of my brain to engage in order to get really turned on. It was interesting, though. I'd never seen so many women naked, so intimately. Their pussies (it really seemed like the right word in this context) were all different, but all... pretty. I found an aesthetic pleasure in looking at them.

I had expected all of the actresses to be shaved bald down there, but most of them had neatly trimmed triangles or lines pointing down, as if to say, "Here it is! Come and get it!"

I liked that.

Behind all of the sets, make-up, and artistry, I found a surprising level of honesty. Between the fake moans, you could see genuine smiles. These women enjoyed their work. You could see it in their eyes. It made me aware that whatever the trappings, I was watching a half-dozen women all really having sex with each other. I wondered what it would be like to live that lifestyle.

There was so much going on so fast in the scene that I had trouble keeping up with it--it was all too new and strange. I hadn't considered myself sheltered, especially after all the things I'd already done this weekend, but I was surprised at the variety of things that I saw just in the first scene of this movie.

The woman with the beautiful head of red hair pushed a double-headed dildo into the brown-haired woman, then started sucking on the other end. It would have never occurred to me to do either of those things. I wondered how it felt.

Another woman pulled out some sort of wand-like vibrator with a massive head on the end. She pushed the head of the device against another woman's clit, while she herself sort of straddled the handle. I tried to picture Jaxon using a toy like that on me, and I got a shiver at the thought of having pleasure relentlessly forced upon me that way.

That ended up being what my mind kept doing during the scene. I kept trying to insert myself into the place of one of the women on the screen, to imagine what it felt like to do what she was doing. In order to do that, I kept trying to mentally replace another woman with Jaxon.

It didn't really work, though. These women were very clearly not male, and Jaxon very clearly was. My brain couldn't make the transposition work.

Jaxon was still looking more at me than at the movie. What was he hoping to find? What reaction was I supposed to be having? Did he want me to feel turned on, or just for me to feel uncomfortable?

As the scene went on, my mind drifted away from the sex. It was like the sex was somehow boring once my brain realized that there wasn't going to be a man in the scene. I started paying more attention to the other details of the scene.

The makeup was more tasteful than I'd expected. The girls generally had a lot more eye shadow than I'd ever use, and some of their lashes seemed overly-long during the close-up shots, but overall things were more subdued than I'd expected, like the makeup artist understood that sometimes less is more.

The costumes were another surprising part. First of all, that they had costumes. I'd have expected a six-girl orgy to be a completely naked affair, but it wasn't. Some of the women were clothed simply in jewelry, like the girl in the oversized ornate gold necklace that covered the upper half of her chest.

One of the blondes was naked other than her high-heels, but she also had a row of tiny little jewels decorating the area underneath each of her eyes. I wondered what it felt like and how they got those things to stick on. The effect was quite pretty.

There were so many little details involved in the scene that once my mind started wandering away from the sex, I spent the rest of the time fixating on all the little things that somebody somewhere must have thought of.

I wondered if Jaxon liked costumes. Then I remembered the clothes that I found in the closet and realized that I already knew the answer. Then I wondered what it would be like to dress up for him, to put on fancy lingerie or a nurse's outfit or whatever.

I realized that my hand had strayed to Jaxon's leg, that it was seeking out his penis underneath the fabric of his pajama pants. I almost pulled my hand away, but then just went with the impulse. I found him, and I started stroking him through the soft fabric.

"Slave," Jaxon addressed me, "what are you thinking right now?"

"Master," I answered honestly, "I was wondering why you would want to watch this movie when you could have the real thing."

A teasing smile crossed his face. "Well, I suppose I could call over a few female friends."

That stung like a slap. I'd been trying to flirt, to get him to say that he'd rather have sex with me than to just sit here watching porn. Okay, I'd been hoping that he'd show me that's what he'd rather do. Instead, he'd deliberately taken my comment the other way, as if I'd been asking him if I could put on a live girl-on-girl show for him.

"Is that what you'd like?" Jaxon idly stroked my bare shoulder as he asked.

My cheeks burned with embarrassment and shame. "No, Master."

I looked away. If that was what he was into, could I ever be enough for him on my own? I'd only ever seen him leave the bar with one girl at a time, but for all I knew he routinely picked up three more on the way home, then had an orgy in this very room while a movie like this played in the background.

The image in my mind was so sleazy that I had to shake my head to clear it. I realized that I'd pulled my hand away from his lap. The thought that I'd need to have sex with other women in order to keep him interested was a splash of cold water on my libido.

I could feel his relentless eyes still on me, trying to force their way into my brain where they could discover all of my secrets. It wasn't fair. I was going to have to tell him my secrets, but there was so much about him that remained a mystery. Why was my guilt at keeping things from him so much stronger than his guilt at keeping things from me?

"How I wish I could get inside of that brain of yours," Jaxon mused. He paused the movie. "What would you like to do right now, if you could do anything?"

Right now? I'd tell Jaxon my secrets. I'd learn as many of his secrets as I could. I'd have sex with Jaxon even though I was a bit hurt at the moment. I'd curl up with him and watch a movie. I'd get rid of the stupid "Master" crap and just hang out with him like a person.

An idea struck me.

"Master," I said. "Have you ever played Truth or Dare?"

For just a moment, Jaxon's face showed a flicker of surprise. I must have astonished him in order for his control to slip that much. I felt myself smiling, pleased that I'd gotten something past his guard.

"Not in quite some time, Slave." He was smiling back at me now, as if he was proud of me, pleased with me, and as if he'd received an unexpected gift. "Truth or Dare it is, then."

# CHAPTER 20

We were back in the main area, in the section that I'd been thinking of as the 'living room,' even though it wasn't actually a separate room. Jaxon had brought out a bottle of champagne because he insisted that the game must be played with alcohol present. He had poured us each a glass.

"Now," Jaxon asked, "who do you think should go first?"

"I'd like to go first, Master." I desperately wanted to know some things about him, and I wanted to put off the moment where I had to tell him about me.

"Nonsense." He dismissed my comment out of hand. "I'm the master. I'll go first. Truth or dare?"

I was caught off guard. I'd already been thinking of what question or dare I'd pose to him, but now I was on the receiving end. I didn't want to jump right into my big revelations, didn't want to risk him asking the wrong thing too early. Maybe this was a mistake. I picked "Dare."

"I dare you to go first." His face was unreadable.

I was getting flustered. I felt like I was losing the game before it even really started. I tried to remember what I'd been planning earlier. I sighed. "Truth or Dare, Master?"

Jaxon looked into my eyes, as if trying to read my thoughts, and then he spoke. "Dare."

I was hoping that he'd pick Truth so that I could ask him why he'd wanted me to watch that movie. I had a backup plan, though, and I thought it was a good one.

"Master, I dare you to free me from the requirement of addressing you as 'Master' for the rest of the day, along with permission to speak freely."

Jaxon cracked a smile. "Granted."

That was a relief. That requirement had kept me in an almost perpetual state of nervousness. I was afraid of slipping up, afraid of getting punished again. This way I could relax a bit and focus on the game. From the way he was playing so far, it seemed like I'd need all of my concentration.

Then I was on the hook again. This time I picked "Truth," hoping that he wouldn't ask a really big question like, "Why are you really here?" or something.

"Slave," Jaxon was still calling me that, even though I didn't have to call him 'master.' Damn. I was hoping we could talk like regular people, but he was sticking to the letter of the dare, not the spirit. "How many men have you had sex with, other than me? 'Sex' in this case referring to oral, vaginal, or anal intercourse."

After Jaxon's insistence on crudity over the weekend, it was odd to hear him say 'intercourse.' If I'd seen this question coming, I'd have expected him to ask how many men I'd 'fucked,' just because he seemed to take such pleasure in making me uncomfortable. I think he was in lawyer-mode, though, using more formal language as a habit.

I hadn't expected that question, and I could feel my cheeks getting red. Jaxon was so experienced, and he was obviously used to experienced women. What would he think of me when I told him how inexperienced I actually was?

"Slave, if you break the rules of the game," Jaxon warned, "I will add the offense to your punishment book."

Oh, shit! I couldn't take another punishment tonight. I was still recovering from the past two nights of it. The fear pushed me into blurting out an honest answer.

"Two, Master." My face felt bright red, my embarrassment made all the worse because I'd accidentally called him 'Master' even though I no longer had to.

Jaxon arched an eyebrow. "Only two men? Truthfully? Tell me about them."

"When I was at community college, there was this guy I kept running into. Jack. We dated, and things started to get serious. Not too serious, but I was eighteen, I thought that I might be in love, and I wanted to know what all the fuss was about, what sex was like. I wanted to know what I was missing out on."

I glanced up at Jaxon. He was listening patiently. I continued.

"After a few weeks, I agreed to go to his place for dinner. I knew what he wanted to happen, and I thought I wanted it, too. It was bad. There was no real foreplay--he barely got me wet, and then just wanted to stick it in. I think he spent more time getting the condom on than he spent inside of me. It was a big disappointment."

"Go on." Jaxon's expression was inscrutable.

"I kind of felt cheated that first time, so we tried again over the next couple of weeks, but it didn't get much better. It never felt special the way that I thought it would. It didn't feel as good as I expected. It didn't let me know what the fuss was about. I dumped him."

"Since there were only two, I'm guessing that the next guy didn't turn out much better?" Jaxon's eyes were narrow and dark. He looked angry. Was he jealous?

"The next guy was Steve, last year. I was trying to…" I'd almost said that I was trying to get over my obsession with Jaxon. I tried to cover it, and to just move on. "Trying to get back into dating. Steve seemed like a good catch. He was a real nice guy, and handsome."

I had more trouble talking about this one. I wasn't sure how to describe what went wrong. I persevered.

"Steve and I dated for a while, and we eventually had sex. He was such a good kisser, and such a good dancer, that I was sure that he'd be good in bed. And I really liked him. So, we... did it."

"You fucked," Jaxon interjected. The sudden crudity stung me a bit, flustered me.

"We had sex." I wasn't going to phrase it Jaxon's way unless he ordered me to. I moved on, before he could have the chance. "And Steve wasn't like Jack. Steve tried really hard. Lots of kissing and foreplay. He was more experienced. He seemed to know what he was doing, and it felt good. It was a lot better than with Jack."

"What happened to Steve, then?" Jaxon looked like a cat who was closing in on a mouse.

"It was me." My face was so red. I hated admitting this. "I couldn't... I just couldn't..."

"He couldn't make you come." Jaxon cut to the chase.

"I couldn't come," I said. "Steve was fine, he tried so hard. I got close, but I just couldn't quite get all the way there. Things would build up, but then they'd just kind of fade away again."

"He couldn't make you come," Jaxon repeated, as if he was correcting me. "Did you fake it?"

I wasn't sure what he meant by that, and I guess he could read the confusion on my face.

"Did you fake your orgasms with Steve?" Jaxon specified.

"No!" I said. "Why would I do that?"

Jaxon nodded.

"That was the thing, everything was pretty good with Steve overall. I was pretty happy, at least, but he couldn't be satisfied unless I had an orgasm. Eventually, he dumped me. He didn't really say why, but I think it's because I wasn't good enough in bed, because I couldn't come for him."

Shit. Now there was a tear forming in the corner of my eye. Jaxon was too good at drawing things out of me. He was supposed to only get one question that I had to answer truthfully, and I'd answered how many now? Enough was enough.

"How many orgasms have you had?" Jaxon asked.

I wiped away the tear and let out a brief laugh.

"Sorry, Jaxon." I deliberately called him by his name instead of 'Master.' "You've had more than one question already. You'll have to save that one for the next Truth."

Jaxon nodded.

"Truth or Dare?" I asked him.

"Truth."

I'd forgotten what I'd wanted to ask him again. I'd been so caught up in my own stuff. I tried not to think about Jack or Steve much. A thought came into my mind, though, a question that I'd burned to know the answer to for a long time, without even really realizing it.

"Jaxon," I said. "Why did you bring me that piece of cake? The one at your birthday party, back when I first started working there?"

Ha! Jaxon seemed to be taken off-guard by that one. His face made funny little movements, just for a heartbeat, then his composure returned.

"You caught my eye," he said. "You were intriguing: a pretty girl in the corner, hiding away from the party. Hiding away from *my* party, when all the other pretty girls were flocking around me, letting me know that I could unwrap their presents any time I wanted. You stood out from the crowd, different from the usual pack of horny gold-diggers."

Was that how he saw the women at the office? It seemed insulting. Then again, I'd heard them talking about him plenty of times, drooling over him. Come to think of it, his money and status invariably came up in those conversations, not just his stunning handsomeness.

I thought that he was exaggerating, but I could see his point of view. I'd never really thought about things from that angle before. A chill ran through me as I thought about how Jaxon might react when he found out the insane lengths I'd gone to in pursuit of him.

He continued speaking, oblivious to my thoughts.

"Of all the women there, you stood out. You needed a friend. You weren't trying to get your hands into my pants or my wallet. You intrigued me."

He looked at me again, piercing my eyes with his, as if he was trying to read my mind. Perhaps he succeeded, but this time I saw something in him as well. Somewhere inside, he was nervous. As controlled as he was on the outside, he'd put himself out on a limb here. He'd revealed something personal.

"Your turn again," Jaxon said.

"Dare."

I felt connected to him, felt safe. That feeling of safety and connection should have prompted me to pick Truth again, but instead it had the opposite effect. I wanted this feeling to continue, and I wasn't sure if it could survive him finding out too much truth too fast.

Jaxon considered for a moment, then he grinned.

"I dare you to shave your pussy. All of it."

Crap. I thought he'd given up on that one. Somehow, though, the idea of it being a dare made it more appealing than if it had been an order. I sighed.

"Right now?"

Jaxon nodded.

I walked off to the bathroom and he followed. I should have known that he'd want to watch.

# CHAPTER 21

Once we were back in the living room again, I tried to return my focus to the game. It was difficult because being hairless down there was distracting. It seemed like I could feel every gentle movement of air in the room now. I hadn't realized that being bare down there would make me feel so utterly naked.

I tried covering myself, crossing my legs, but my body was so used to the protection that my hair had offered me that now even the touch of my own flesh against that newly denuded region was startlingly sensual.

Jaxon had watched the entire process. He didn't touch me, even after I had finished, but there was a hunger in his eyes when he looked at me. I felt naked, sensual, and attractive.

"Truth or Dare?" I asked Jaxon.

He picked Dare again. Damn. There was still so much that I wanted to know, so much that I couldn't wait to ask. On the other hand, I had no shortage of Dares for him either.

I felt so naked now, and he still had on his pajama pants. It wasn't fair.

"I dare you to be naked for the rest of the day."

The corners of his mouth turned slightly down at that, as if he didn't like equalizing things. Tough.

"You again." Jaxon took his pants, folded them, and set them on a nearby table.

"Dare." I wanted to get back to the Truths, but right now I was feeling sexy, and I wanted to see what he'd dare me to do next, now that we were both naked.

He didn't hesitate. "I dare you to crawl for me. To the kitchen and back."

Man, he didn't let go of anything.

I crawled. Like with the shaving, it helped that this was a dare instead of a command. As I crawled, my inner thighs rubbed over my newly bare flesh, making me shiver and tingle with pleasure. I looked back at one point. I could see Jaxon staring at my ass. I wondered how much he could see of my pussy. Somehow, now that it was completely shaved, the word "pussy" came more readily to my mind.

As I slowly crawled back toward him, Jaxon watched my breasts jiggle and slightly sway with each movement. By the time I crawled to the floor in front of him, he was hard. I was getting wet from the movements, and from the way he was looking at me.

Crawling might not be so bad if it had this effect every time.

"Truth," Jaxon said, without waiting for me to ask. I'd been hoping he'd ask for another Dare, because the way I was feeling, I had a few things in mind.

While I was crawling, I'd remembered something else I'd wanted to ask him.

"Why are my clothes in your closet?"

He looked puzzled. "What do you mean?"

"In the closet of that bedroom," I pointed in the general direction. "You have a bunch of my outfits. I saw them when I was picking out a coat and shoes the other day. Why do you have my clothes?"

Jaxon smiled, almost laughed. He also turned slightly pink. He was the embarrassed one for a change.

"Ah." He seemed to be trying to find the best way to explain things. After a pause, he said: "They're not actually your clothes."

"Jaxon, I recognize my own clothing."

"No…" Jaxon looked at the floor, off to the side of where I was sitting. "I mean, they're the same type of clothes, but you've never worn them."

I just looked at him.

"When I have slaves here, for the weekend..." This was the most uncomfortable I'd ever seen him. Part of me felt victorious, but part of me was worried what he was going to say next.

He almost mumbled the next part. I would never have imagined Jaxon Kent ever mumbling anything. "Sometimes I like them to dress up."

"What?" I didn't know what he was saying. I really didn't. I mean, I could hear the words, but I couldn't fathom a meaning.

He brushed the back of his head with his hand, looking uncomfortable. "You know. Role-playing stuff. Sexy nurses and stuff. A police woman who gets trapped in her own cuffs. That sort of thing."

I just let him continue. I didn't see where he was going with this. My brain kept circling around an answer but it was too shy to close in for the kill, to commit to actually thinking that thought.

"Secretaries...French maids…." He was circling in on something himself. Then he went calm, the kind of relaxed look a person might get when they gave up on being embarrassed and just opened themselves up completely. He looked right at me, his eyes both impaling and open.

"You," he spoke softly, but with the strength that comes from earnestness. "Sometimes I'd dress my slaves up as you."

I felt dizzy. I had been sitting upright, but now I leaned over to one side, supporting myself with my arms. Me. Jaxon had dressed his slave girls up to look like me. He had noticed what I was wearing, bought imitations of my outfits, and he had put those outfits on his Mayflowers.

I knew that he'd been having sex with his slaves. I never dreamed that when he was having sex with them, that he'd even once been thinking of me. Jaxon had been fucking me by proxy, had been sticking his cock in those beautiful girls, and he'd been pretending that he was sticking himself into me.

I hated the thought of him being with other women. I hated the thought that they'd been the wet receptacles for his passion. But my heart rejoiced at the thought that he'd fantasized about me that way, to that extent.

I should have found it creepy, I guess. If it had been anybody but Jaxon, just a random co-worker that I'd discovered was dressing women up to look like me in order to have sex with them... I'd have been disgusted, offended. Probably.

With Jaxon, though, it just made me melt. Instead of finding his behavior creepy, it just felt like my own actions were a bit less creepy. I'd been hopelessly obsessed with him, but he'd also been obsessed with me.

It must have cost him a lot to tell me that. It must have felt like such a risk for him to get found out. I wanted to tell him that it was okay, that I understood. I wanted to tell him so much, so fast, that there just weren't words.

So instead I got off of the floor, and I kissed him.

It was a long, deep kiss of frantic passion. I caught him off-guard, my tongue slipping into his mouth as my hands wrapped around his head. He kissed me back, and we lost ourselves in each other for a while.

The kissing eventually slowed, then stopped. I pulled back, and I looked at him. I looked at this man who had been quietly interested in me, perhaps even fascinated or obsessed with me.

"I guess you don't mind, then?" He smiled at me, a look of relief and wonder on his face.

"I had no idea you even thought about me like that," I said.

"Truth or Dare?" Jaxon cut off my unasked questions.

I thought about it. If he could make that confession, I could tell him anything.

"Truth."

"How many women have you had sex with? Again, 'sex' refers to oral, anal, or vaginal intercourse."

I was a bit shocked. "None."

Jaxon nodded, as if I'd confirmed something.

"Your turn to ask me." He seemed anxious to get on with the game, as if he had a lot more questions.

"Truth or Dare?"

"Truth," he said.

"You had those women dress like me. You found me intriguing on that first day, on your birthday, when you gave me cake. Why didn't you ever just ask me out?"

"I didn't think you'd be interested." He seemed to find the question annoying, as if I should already know the answer. "I didn't think that you'd share my particular sexual tastes and hobbies. I assumed that you were vanilla, and that you'd find my interests... well, horrifying. You never showed any strong interest in me, not until I literally bumped into you in the bar the other night."

Oh. I guess I hadn't. I'd tried to keep things in control, tried not to show my hand, but part of me somehow felt like he'd always known anyway, that I'd felt so strongly about him that he couldn't help but know. I guess that part of me had been wrong.

"Truth or Dare?" He asked. "Choose Dare."

"Dare." I wasn't sure of the point of the game if he was going to make the decisions for me, but I trusted him.

"I dare us both to have a glass of champagne, without speaking again until we are done drinking."

That was odd. On the other hand, I felt like I could use a drink. My heart wasn't racing, but it was beating faster than normal. I felt anxious, tense. I wondered if Jaxon felt the same way.

Jaxon poured us each a glass of champagne and we drank in silence, each of us occasionally looking at each other, but mostly just staring off to the side, lost in our own thoughts. I couldn't speak for Jaxon, but I needed that. I had a lot of thoughts.

I still couldn't believe that Jaxon had his sex slaves dress up like me. I kept flashing back to his closet, though, and in hindsight it was pretty undeniable. There had been costume after costume, then clothing that looked like mine. No outfits from any of the other women at the office, just me. Jaxon was only interested in me that way, to that level.

Well, me and generic fantasy nurses and nuns and such.

I was one of Jaxon's fantasies. That was so strange. I'd never been the fantasy for a man before, especially not the fantasy for a man whom I was fantasizing about.

I was starting to get scared. Not just scared that I'd fucked things up by messing up our beginning, and not just scared at how Jaxon would react when I told him my secrets. Now I was scared that this would somehow all work out, that Jaxon and I could make this work in the long run.

I'd been alone so long that successful romance was frightening and unknown to me.

After a time, we finished our drinks. The alcohol was already kicking in, making me feel more relaxed. I was glad. I needed it.

Jaxon finished first. Once my empty glass joined his glass on the coffee table, it was my turn to challenge Jaxon again. This time he chose Dare.

I had to think about it. My mind was working slowly, still processing all the new information. I picked a fantasy at random, and went with it. The alcohol made me brave enough to say what I wanted.

"I dare you to watch a movie with me later. A normal movie, like we're boyfriend and girlfriend, not porn."

Jaxon shrugged. "Accepted."

Then I was up again.

"Dare," I said.

"I dare you to sign the weeklong contract with me."

I couldn't believe it! It was what I wanted. Well, one of the things that I wanted. Couldn't he just want a normal relationship?

It was too soon, though. I had more to tell him first. I had to come clean before we could move forward.

"Truth," I said.

Jaxon raised his eyebrows. "Okay. Truth, then. Why don't you want to sign the weeklong contract with me?"

I wanted to blurt it all out, but it wasn't right. He hadn't asked the right question the right way, and there was some kind of mental lock on my mouth that kept me from just spilling everything. That lock needed the right key, and this wasn't it. But it would get us closer.

"There's something I need to tell you first."

"Okay," Jaxon said. "What do you need to tell me first?"

I shook my head. "No, that was your one question. My turn now. Truth or Dare?"

Jaxon seemed annoyed, but he let it go. "Truth."

"Why are you so interested in..." I wasn't sure how to phrase it, but I'd already started asking.

"You asked me how many women I'd been with. You had me watch lesbian porn earlier. You hinted that you could invite other women over, watch me be with them. Why? Is that what you want? You want to see me have sex with other girls?"

"No." Jaxon's mouth made a smile that looked like a frown. "I mean, yes, I like to watch women having sex with each other. I like having sex with two or more women at once. I am into that kind of thing. It's not what I want specifically from you, though. I was testing you."

"Testing me? For what?" I said my thoughts aloud.

"There have been clues, mostly little clues, all over the place. One of the big clues was when you told Stacy--the girl in the store--that you'd never paddled anybody before."

Uh-oh. I suddenly thought that I knew where this was going.

"That was a clue," Jaxon said. "Because Mistress Sophie always trains all her slaves to use the paddle. She always makes sure that her slaves know what punishment feels like from both ends. Before they can be paddled, they have to use a paddle. Before they can be whipped, they have to use a whip. So either you were lying to me or you were telling the truth. And if you were telling the truth about never using a paddle before, that meant that you were lying about something else: Mistress Sophie didn't send you."

Oh, shit. Shit, shit, shit.

"The girl/girl stuff was just confirming what I already knew, because all of Mistress Sophie's girls like to play with other women. That's why they're with her, after all."

There was anger on his face, in his eyes. It had probably been building for some time, but now he was letting it out. It wasn't a burning rage, it was something worse. It was cold. Those blue eyes of his looked like ice, and I could feel a chill in my soul as those icy eyes of his locked onto me.

"Jaxon, I..." I started to try to explain. He knew. Of course he knew. I felt a cold knot of anxiety in my stomach. I felt like I was going to vomit.

"No." Jaxon cut me off. His smile was cruel, as cool as his eyes. "No, you're right. We're playing this game. You asked me a question; I answered. You don't get to answer anything until it comes up again. Truth or Dare?"

"Truth!" I was miserable. I just wanted to come clean, about everything. I wanted him to ask me.

His grin turned sadistic, and instead he asked, "How many times a week do you normally masturbate?"

"None." I looked at the floor. He was going to prolong this, drag it out further. I'd done the same thing, but I hadn't known that he was onto me. I thought I was making things easier, and he knew that he was making them harder. He really was a sadist. "Truth or Dare?"

"Dare," he said.

"I dare you to punish me for lying to you."

My voice was soft, but strong. I meant it. I wanted this to be over. I was still so sore from the flogging, and from the paddling, and from the spankings. I didn't want another punishment, but if I had wanted it, then it wouldn't really be punishment. Besides, nothing could be worse than feeling how I felt right then: caught, trapped, humiliated, and worthless.

"Accepted." Jaxon sounded slightly mollified, but only slightly. "But I can't punish you until after I know exactly what your lies were, and why you told them."

"Truth," I said.

I didn't wait for him to go through the motions of the game.

"Why are you here?"

# CHAPTER 22

Why was I here? That was the question. That was what I needed to answer. The problem was that I didn't exactly know. I decided to just start talking, to let myself go and to see where I'd end up.

"You've been fantasizing about me."

I started off with the facts, stating them for the record. It sounded so weird, saying it aloud. "You've been so intrigued by me, so attracted to me that you've dressed other women up to look like me while you had sex with them."

Jaxon waited, as if I'd been talking about the weather and he'd rather I get to the point.

"I've fantasized about you too." It felt horrible and freeing to say it. I was starting to blush again and felt incredibly self-conscious, but I said it, and it was true. "I've thought about you, about being with you, since the day we met. You probably don't even remember, but there was that one day where I accidently walked in on you when you were changing shirts? I've thought about it, a lot. I've had fantasies of you taking me, bending me over your desk, ripping off my panties, and... well. I've had fantasies."

Jaxon's face was inscrutable, a perfectly impenetrable mask covering his reactions to my words. But his cock was getting hard

"I've wanted you for so long." My lips were dry. I licked them. "I've longed for you. I never thought it could happen, because workplace romance is a no-no, and because I never thought that a man like you could fall for a girl like me."

Still hardening. I was appealing to his ego and to his interest in me. Better still, I was doing it honestly. Every word I said was the naked truth.

"I got kind of…" I didn't want to say the word. I had to say the word, though. There wasn't anything else that would be as true. "I got a bit obsessed with you as time went on, as I got to know you. I tried to find out about your love life, about any girls that you were dating."

"I see." Jaxon's face was a mask. His cock was at half-mast, still growing slightly.

"I found out that you were into kinky stuff, things that a normal girl wouldn't ever go for. I found out about the Mayflowers. Not much, just that you were with a different one every week, that they were into the same things that you were, and that they were 'slaves.'"

"How'd you find out about them? How much do you know?" Jaxon seemed wary, as if he was afraid that I was a spy or something.

I shook my head. "We're still playing the game. You'll have to ask those questions later. Let me finish."

Jaxon rolled his eyes, but nodded his head in agreement.

"I've always…" I searched for the words. "I've had problems with self-control. Sometimes I know what the right thing is, and I just do the wrong thing anyway. Friday night, I'd had too much to drink. My self-control slipped, and when I bumped into you in the hallway, my mouth just kind of took over."

"I'd fantasized about you so long, wanted you for so long that I just couldn't help myself." We were both standing now. I felt myself take a step closer to him. "I offered myself to you by posing as a Mayflower. I didn't think that you'd accept. I mean I wasn't really thinking at all, but I didn't imagine that you'd want a normal girl like me, not with everything I knew about your sex life."

Jaxon laughed out loud.

"What?" I asked.

He just kept laughing. I don't think that he could stop himself. I'd never seen him lose control like that before, never seen him break down into such honest, unexpected emotion. But I couldn't shake the feeling that he was laughing at *me*.

"Oh, no!" His eyes danced with utter amusement. "Oh, no. we're still playing the game, remember? If you want to know why, why I'm laughing, then you'll just have to ask me next turn."

"Fine. Truth or Dare? Pick Truth." I glared at him, daring him to pick Dare instead.

"Truth."

"Why are you laughing at me?"

"It's what you just said." Jaxon shrugged, then elaborated. "I've met people with an inaccurate self-image before, but you? You take the cake."

"What?" I was angry, confused. "Why?"

"Stasia, you stalked me. You lied your way into my home by pretending to be my sex slave. You've let me beat you and fuck you six ways til Tuesday, and even though you are---no offense--a complete sexual novice, I didn't really catch on for sure until today."

He was laughing again.

"So?"

"So," Jaxon managed to bring his laugh down to a chuckle. "I think you really, really have to let go of this idea that you're a 'normal girl.'"

Oh. Put like that, I saw his point.

I cracked a smile. The smile broke into a grin. Then I was laughing with him. It felt good, cathartic. I was laughing so hard that I had to lean on him for support, but we were naked so the next thing I knew, we were kissing again, our hands roaming around each other's bodies.

I felt that charge building up inside of me, that sexual charge like the air before a storm. I felt giddy, and alive, and happy. We hadn't resolved anything, but it felt like we'd accomplished something even if I couldn't say exactly what.

The kissing and touching became groping and fondling. I could tell that we were headed toward sex, which would feel good, but I didn't feel like we'd covered everything that we needed to.

I looked at Jaxon. "Let's just do Truth for a bit. Let's set the game aside, and just tell each other everything. Ask me something. Anything."

Jaxon asked me something, but his voice was muffled by a mouthful of my breast. I gently pulled his head away, and told him to ask again.

"Why the hell didn't you just say the safe word? Or let me know sooner what the hell was going on?"

"That first night I was a bit drunk, and I wasn't thinking straight. After I'd lied at the bar, it would have been humiliating to explain what I'd done, that I'd pretended to be a slave sent to you for the weekend. So I just played along."

"You just played along." Jaxon looked like he was close to laughing again. There was something else in his eyes, something like pride. "You just played along, pretending to be a level seven, even though you didn't know what one was. You just played along, while I collared you… Christ, no wonder you didn't want to crawl around on the leash. You've never been leash-broken. You just played along while I spanked you, tore your clothing, paddled you, and molested you."

I wanted to be completely honest. "I didn't want to say the safe word because I couldn't stand the thought of you never speaking to me again. That's what got me through the early parts."

"A normal girl would have *begged* for me to never speak to her again after I started spanking her."

Jaxon was looking at me with admiration. "You are a fucking marvel. That rule, though--the never-speaking thing--it's just part of the spiel. After I broke my rule about never taking in a girl from the office, I probably should have dropped it. But I was pretty drunk myself, and it just didn't occur to me."

Jaxon was drunk that night? I'd had no idea. I was a bit out of it myself, but he'd seemed stone cold sober, like always.

"My God," Jaxon said, "if we'd both been a bit more sober, this wouldn't have happened. You wouldn't have tried to con your way in, I wouldn't have fallen for it. I wouldn't have broken my rule about the workplace... well, no. That part's not true."

Jaxon captured me with his eyes, then said: "I probably would have broken that rule anyway, for you."

I melted a little. I didn't know what to say. That was alright, because Jaxon kept talking.

"I would have picked up on more clues. I mean, I guessed that you were lying about being a level seven--a seven would have picked the cane--but I might have fit together all the pieces of the puzzle a lot sooner. So you never said the safe word, even through all of that, because you couldn't stand to never talk to me again?"

"Well," I felt the need to be completely honest. "I was going to say it anyway, but then you made me come. I'd never had an orgasm before."

Jaxon looked at me, incredulous. Then he grabbed the hair on the back of my head, and he pulled me in for a long kiss.

"Well, damn," he said. "That must have been one hell of a first date for you!"

I nodded. Then we just kind of stood there for a few moments. I wasn't sure what to do next, so I proposed having more champagne. Jaxon readily agreed and refilled our glasses. We drank in silence again, each absorbed in our own thoughts.

When our glasses were empty once more, I broke the silence.

"If you want me to sign a weeklong contract," I said. "I will. I'll do it. But... can't we just start, you know... dating? Just have a normal relationship, without contracts and stuff?"

"Stasia, I've tried normal before." Jaxon looked at me and gave me a wicked grin. "It just doesn't work for me, doesn't give me what I need. How's it worked out for you?"

It hasn't, I thought. I've never had a normal relationship that was anywhere close to successful. All my life, I'd wondered why I couldn't just find my prince and my happily-ever-after. Maybe I'd been looking in the wrong places.

I remembered that tarot card reading from so long ago, remembered the pictures on the cards. The Prince of Wands, my prince, didn't have a shining sword for slaying dragons. My prince had a stout wooden rod. That reminded me of something.

"Jaxon," I said, "will the entire week be like this? Will it all be like this weekend?"

"Good Lord, no!" Jaxon laughed. "I mean, sometimes it will be, but during the week things would be much more relaxed. What we've been up to, that's the intense stuff. It's what I live for, but it's not the kind of thing that anybody can do all day, every day."

I was relieved.

"There are physical limitations, for one thing. The flesh is sturdy, but it has limits. I'd love to paddle you every day if I could, but the simple fact is that too much paddling too often can cause long-term damage. The body needs time to heal now and then."

"Oh, thank God!" I blurted out. "I'm so sore today that it hurts to sit down. After you... punish me for lying, I think I could really use a day off."

Jaxon nodded. "More than that. I think we should wait until tomorrow for your punishment. Now that I know you're not used to this, I think we should probably let you heal a little before we do any more serious stuff. You don't know your own limits, and sometimes subs can let themselves get hurt by agreeing to too much punishment."

I was glad that he wanted to give me more time, but something occurred to me.

"Tomorrow is Monday," I pointed out. "What if I don't sign the contract?"

Jaxon looked at me. "If you don't sign the contract, you're no longer my slave, and I will not punish you."

So if I decided to stay with him, I was going to get flogged or beaten in some way. If I decided to let him go, to try to move on and find somebody normal, then this would be over. I wouldn't have to be spanked, paddled, or whipped ever again.

"I see what you're doing," I said.

"What?" Jaxon gave an innocent smile that I could see right through.

"You're testing me again. If I sign the contract, I get punished. If I don't, then I can't be with you. You're setting things up where I'll effectively be punished for choosing you."

"Perhaps." Jaxon's face was unreadable, but I was confident that I was right.

"You're trying to see if I want to be with you enough to suffer through pain that I don't have to take on." I stepped forward, put my arms around him. "But we both already know the answer to that, because I'm here."

I looked at him. He was so damned handsome that I couldn't believe he was real, that he was with me. I could feel our naked bodies pressed against each other, feel the hard muscles of his shoulders with my forearms. My fingers were laced behind his neck. I pulled him in for a quick kiss.

"I dare you..." I started to speak, but Jaxon interrupted me.

"Wait a minute." His arms were around my waist, pulling our bodies even closer together. His penis was pressed up against my belly. He was starting to get hard. "Is it even your turn? And weren't we sticking with Truths for a while?"

"Just listen." There was a hint of a plea in my voice, my sudden desperation leaking out. "I dare you to make love to me."

"Oh," he said. "In that case..."

His hands moved lower and cupped my buttocks. I could feel the power in his hands, the strength of them. My knees trembled a bit, and my longing for him increased.

"I dare you to make love to me," I clarified, "like normal couples do. Nothing kinky. Let's just make love."

Jaxon frowned a bit. He sighed. "Dare accepted."

The next thing I knew, Jaxon's hands had slipped lower, and he was grabbing the backs of my thighs. Then I was falling, my legs pulled out from under me. Jaxon still had ahold of me and I still had ahold of his neck, so it was a controlled fall. I landed gently with my back on the thick white carpet in front of the couch.

Jaxon was on top of me. He had pulled my legs apart as he pulled them out from under me, and Jaxon was lying between my thighs. I could feel the heat of his erection pressed against my newly-bare pubic mound.

I gasped from surprise and sensation. Those private places that had been protected by hair were now completely open, vulnerable, and highly sensitive. I felt my hips move, felt my body stroking itself against Jaxon's length. I wanted him inside of me.

Instead, Jaxon kissed me briefly on the lips, then on the chin, then my throat. He kissed my chest, between my breasts, then moved on to kiss each breast and nipple. He continued to trail kisses down my body, shifting his position as he went.

That naked, aching place between my thighs felt Jaxon's shaft slide lower and lower along my flesh, until it vanished from my sense of touch entirely, and my mound was instead caressing first the hard ridges of Jaxon's stomach, then the muscles of Jaxon's chest, and then the trail of kisses brought Jaxon's head between my legs, and I felt his mouth on me.

He didn't dive straight for the clitoris like I was longing for. Instead he placed a series of kisses in circles around my center. Without any hair there to warn me, to protect me, it was a bit like being blindfolded-- every touch of his lips on my skin was an ambush on my senses. Every ambush made my body strain all the more to anticipate, and that anticipation made each assault on me all the more intense when it happened.

I could feel how wet I was getting. My hips were moving in circles, trying to trap his mouth into touching that place where I needed it most. Jaxon shifted his shoulders, moving them first between and then under my thighs, until my legs were pushed up into the air.

He reached around the outside of my body, grabbing my wrists, trapping them. As soon as I was helpless, he pounced. His mouth dove toward my center, and his tongue was on my clit.

I fought off a moan of pleasure. "Jaxon, no. Let go of my wrists. Nothing kinky, remember?"

Jaxon let go of my wrists, moving his hands instead to my breasts, squeezing them. My hips pushed against his mouth, and I sank back in a wash of relaxed bliss. This time I didn't fight it; I let out a loud moan.

Jaxon's tongue continued to tease me, torment me. He tasted every part of me, licking every crease and crevice he could find. He found them all.

While his tongue worked me over, his hands stayed busy as well. He pinched my nipples, squeezed and caressed my breasts. His hands ran over my sides and my belly, glided over my hips, and squeezed my ass. Every place he touched my skin, I felt a glow of pleasure.

My entire body was alive with the pleasure of his touch, except for the one place where I needed him most.

"I want you inside of me." The words came out between a series of gasps, as his tongue teased some sweet and secret spot.

Jaxon kept licking. I wrapped my fingers around the back of his head, first pulling him in closer, then guiding him away. He relented, moving his body into position, kneeling between my thighs and aligning himself into position.

Instead of thrusting inside of me, he continued to tease me. He moved his cock up and down my slit, brushing it over my clit, then dipping back down to my entrance. I moved my hips, trying to catch him, trying to impale myself on him, but he continued the slow torture until I was begging him to take me.

Then he gave me what I yearned for. He slid inside of me, all of him. I was so ready for him that I felt a jolt of near-orgasmic pleasure shoot through me when he entered, and again with each and every stroke he made.

His chest was pressed against mine, and I wrapped my arms and legs around him. Little sparks of pain danced across my still-sore ass as it moved against the rug, but I didn't mind. It added a bit of extra spice.

Jaxon's pubic hair tickled my hairless flesh each time he penetrated me. I had never felt so naked before during sex, and I really enjoyed it. I was glad that I'd taken that particular dare, and I wondered what it would feel like if we were both naked down there.

Jaxon felt so huge inside of me, like he was filling me up completely. I'd never felt so stretched and satisfied. He was so big.

"You are so tight!" Jaxon said. His smile turned into a kiss, and his tongue probed my mouth.

I matched his movements with my own, our bodies dancing together in a timeless rhythm. Time seemed to fade, and I lost myself to the sheer sensuality of our lovemaking. Pleasure blossomed inside of me, and I felt myself getting closer and closer to orgasm.

The impending explosion of my senses kept building and building, but then it plateaued, and I couldn't quite get there. It was like having a word on the tip of your tongue that you can't remember, only instead of a word, it was a world of bliss.

Jaxon kept moving inside of me, and time slowly returned. I could feel him throb inside of me. I could feel his movements become more cautious. He was holding off on his own pleasure until I came, but I couldn't quite get there.

Pleasure started to turn to frustration, and I cried out, "Smack me."

"What?" Jaxon gave me a surprised smile.

"Slap my breasts. I need it to push me over."

"You want me to slap your tits? Say it."

"I want you to slap my tits!" That last word came through gritted teeth. Jaxon somehow knew the words I objected to, and he forced me to use them.

As soon as the words left my mouth, Jaxon's arm was in motion, as if it had been spring-loaded this whole time, just waiting to strike. His palm struck the side of my breast, sending it bouncing.

The sensation rocked me, adding to the pleasure that had been building up. I was almost there.

"Again. Do it again!" I said.

His hand found my other breast, his fingertips stinging my nipple. Then his palm found that first breast again, stinging my soft flesh with his strength.

"Come!" He was giving me an order, not a request. His voice, uttering that single word, combined with the sting in my breasts and the pleasure in the rest of my body, was enough to send me rocketing over the edge into orgasm, into oblivion.

I started to come, and I couldn't stop coming. Jaxon was still sliding in and out of me, still pumping me full of pleasure to the point of bursting. He was still holding off, delaying his own moment of ecstasy in order to prolong mine.

My moment turned into moments, as the pleasure just continued to sweep through me. I shouted out rough, hoarse, primal cries. I lost full control of my limbs. My fingers clawed his back, my nails scraped his skin.

Then Jaxon came, and we were coming together, lost in pleasure, lost in each other. Jaxon cried out, and kept crying out as his movements reached a frantic peak. I could feel him jet his warmth inside of me, and his movements and cries started to slow. They grew slower and slower, like a steam train approaching a station. Eventually they stopped, and he just lay there, on top of me and inside of me.

I was crying. It wasn't that I was sad, just that I was overwhelmed. The pleasure that Jaxon brought me was always intense, and it always came with an inexplicable rainbow of emotions, possibly even memories.

I was incredibly happy, but I was also sad. I felt a loss inside of me, because I had finally, completely let go of something that I'd clung to for far too long. I had been the one to break. I had been the one who needed the violence. I had been the one who asked Jaxon to hit me this time.

I was too giddy in afterglow to care about that, and I doubted that I'd really care when I came down from the sexual high. I understood myself better now. I wasn't quite sure what I was, what set of labels might apply to me, but I finally understood that I wasn't really normal after all.

I simply wasn't wired the normal way, and that was a big reason why normal relationships had never worked for me. I was abnormal, and I was finally able to accept that. More than accept it-- I reveled in it.

But it was still a loss.

It was still a part of me that was gone, or that I finally realized was never even there. My world was changed now, and it could never go back to the way it was. Not that I wanted it to.

Jaxon smiled at my tears as if he understood, and perhaps he did. Maybe not fully, but I believe that he got the gist of what was happening, that I was moving on from my former life, moving into the kind of life that he had. The kind of life that he wanted to share with me.

# CHAPTER 23

Afterward, we showered. We soaped each other up and rinsed each other off. The process of washing each other was stimulating enough that once we were done, we ended up on the bed together, and we had sex again.

Then we showered again.

Once we finally achieved that perfect blend of satiety and cleanliness, we went back to the entertainment room and watched a movie together. It was a proper movie, not porn. It was something with zombies, I think. Or maybe a serial killer. It's hard to remember--we've watched so many movies since.

It was a horror film, though. I remember that. I remember jumping with fright, clinging to Jaxon's muscular body for protection. I remember feeling perfectly safe in his arms.

After that movie came another movie, then dinner. After dinner, we talked some more. We dispensed with the games. No more Truth or Dare, not now anyway. We just talked like we'd talked countless times before, only more freely, more intimately.

I found out that Jaxon had planned for me to walk in on him, that first time I saw him without a shirt. He laughed when he told me, said that he'd been standing there for nearly ten minutes before I finally arrived. When I didn't use the opportunity to try to seduce him, he assumed that I wasn't interested.

He never knew the effect that he'd had on me.

We slept together in the master bed that night, in Jaxon's bed. He'd never allowed a slave to sleep with him there before, but then, as he said himself, I was more than just a slave.

I signed the contract the next morning. Jaxon went to work after breakfast, and I stayed at his place, relaxing and healing, resting up for the night's punishment. Jaxon had already written it down in his book.

When Jaxon finally came home at the end of the day, I greeted him, naked and kneeling, just inside the green doors. I was wearing my collar, though. I never wanted to take it off.

Before he even removed his coat, I had his pants unzipped, and I had his cock in my mouth. I kept him there until he came, and I swallowed his seed happily, although I laughed a lot inside my head when I mentally called it that.

I didn't worry about my own orgasm that time. I just wanted to please him, and I knew that he'd take very, very good care of me later. Which he did.

When the time came for my punishment, Jaxon again cuffed me to that large table. I was trapped. I was naked and helpless, completely at Jaxon's mercy. It was starting to feel like home.

Jaxon did have some mercy, it seemed, because this time he gave me three choices for my punishment. First he laid down the cane right where I could see it. A shiver of fear went down my spine.

Next, he lay down that black paddle. I remembered how it had felt, how it had left bruises, bruises that were still fading.

Finally, he lay down a large pink feather. He was giving me an out. He was letting me know that even though he technically had to punish me, he was willing to take it very easy on me if that was what I wanted.

I laughed at him, and I chose the cane.

I wanted this to be completely over. I wanted to have the slate washed so completely clean between us that not only would Jaxon truly feel like I had atoned for my mistakes, but I also had to be sure that I would feel that way myself.

No matter how things ended up between us in the long run, I didn't ever want to look back at how we started and feel even a shred of guilt.

Jaxon nodded gravely, but there was a twinkle in his eyes. He slowly picked up the cane and walked out of my field of vision. I could hear his footsteps approaching behind me.

Then I could hear the cane swishing through the air, again and again, as Jaxon took his practice swings. I just wanted it over with. The anticipation was terrible. The anticipation was wonderful.

Just when I started to relax, just when I started to get used to the sound, that's when the next swish ended with a mighty crack. The next moments were lost to searing pain.

As soon as the pain and screaming started to recede, Jaxon struck again.

Then it again, for a third time.

It was the worst experience of my life. It was worse than all the guilt that I'd ever felt about wronging Jaxon. It was worse than all the guilt that I'd ever felt combined.

It was what I wanted, and I've never, ever looked back.

# ABOUT KELLI ROBERTS

Kelli Roberts is an author, webmaster and AVN nominated producer who has worked in the adult industry since 1996.

You can learn more about her books at book.kelli.net.

During her time in the adult industry as an adult entertainment strategy consultant she has worked with several well-known companies including FreeOnes, Cezar Capone, Bluebird Films, Amateur District, Porn Authority, Pornstar.com, Gamelink, AdultDVD.com, and more.

She wrote and produced her first adult movie in 2010 – *Hocus Pocus XXX* which went on to be nominated for 3 AVN awards.

You can keep up with Kelli's latest books at book.kelli.net or you can follow her on twitter @MissKelliXXX or on Google+ at google.com/+KelliRoberts.

If you've enjoyed her work you can join her newsletter so that she can update you about future projects at book.kelli.net. She also offers a free story exclusively to those who subscribe to her newsletter.

# ABOUT RICHARD BACULA

Richard Bacula has always been interested in two things - storytelling and sex. When he was a child he wrote stories full of longing--a yearning for something more--a door to Narnia, a magic sword, a spaceship to a distant land. As an adult, his stories grew, evolved, and became more about the ecstasy and escape of relationships, about the doorway of endless possibilities that love and sex bring to the human experience.

Through his writing, he has found a way to share the strange worlds inside his own head with other people, his readers. These worlds vary from more mundane sexual encounters such as a young man and his female barber in "An Innocent Haircut," to his more sophisticated takes on exotic sub-genres, as with his stories "Satisfied by a Stegosaurus," "Moonheat," and "Corn Hold."

You can follow Richard on twitter @RichardBacula.

# ABOUT WASTELAND.COM

Launched by AVN Hall of Fame inductees Colin Rowntree and Angie Rowntree (founder of Sssh.com) in 1994, Wasteland.com is one of the web's oldest and longest-running adult entertainment sites, and remains the premier online destination for authentic BDSM content.

With an archive of exclusive photos and videos comprising nearly 20 years of regular updates, in addition to an enormous collection of high quality third-party content, Wasteland.com is also among the largest collections of BDSM materials ever assembled.

A tech-forward enterprise since its inception, Wasteland.com has expanded to include Virtual Wasteland.com and Wasteland3d.com, interactive virtual porn properties that enable fans and members to create their own scenarios, working with a wide variety of environments, accessories and functions enabled by the systems' sophisticated back-end software platform.

Made in the USA
San Bernardino, CA
31 October 2015